By Eudora Welty

THE WIDE NET

THE
WIDE NET

AND OTHER STORIES

BY

EUDORA WELTY

A HARVEST BOOK
HARCOURT BRACE & COMPANY
San Diego   New York   London

Requests for permission to make copies
of any part of the work should be mailed to:
Permissions Department,
Harcourt Brace & Company, 6277 Sea Harbor Drive,
Orlando, Florida 32887-6777.

Library of Congress Cataloging-in-Publication Data
Welty, Eudora, 1909–
The wide net and other stories.
(A Harvest Book)
Contents: First love.—The wide net.—
A still moment.—
I. Title.
PZ3.W4696Wi5 [PS3545.E6] 813'.5'2 73-12880

ISBN 0-15-696610-7

Printed in the United States of America

K M N L J

To My Mother,
Chestina Andrews Welty

For permission to reprint the stories in this collection the author wishes to thank the editors of the *Atlantic Monthly, Harper's Bazaar, Harper's Magazine, American Prefaces, Tomorrow,* and the *Yale Review*

CONTENTS

THE WIDE NET

FIRST LOVE

*W*HATEVER happened, it happened in extraordinary times, in a season of dreams, and in Natchez it was the bitterest winter of them all. The north wind struck one January night in 1807 with an insistent penetration, as if it followed the settlers down by their own course, screaming down the river bends to drive them further still. Afterwards there was the strange drugged fall of snow. When the sun rose the air broke into a thousand prisms as close as the flash-and-turn of gulls' wings. For a long time afterwards it was so clear that in the evening the little companion-star to Sirius could be seen plainly in the heavens by travelers who took their way by night, and Venus shone in the daytime in all its course through the new transparency of the sky.

The Mississippi shuddered and lifted from its bed, reaching like a somnambulist driven to go in new places; the ice stretched far out over the waves. Flatboats and rafts continued to float downstream, but with unsignalling passengers submissive and huddled, mere bundles of sticks; bets were laid on shore as to whether they were alive or dead, but it was impossible to prove it either way.

The coated moss hung in blue and shining garlands over the trees along the changed streets in the morning. The town of little galleries was all laden roofs and silence. In the fastness of Natchez it began to seem then that the whole world, like itself, must be in a transfiguration. The only clamor came from the animals that suffered in their stalls, or from the wildcats that howled in closer rings each night from the frozen cane. The Indians could be heard from greater distances and in greater numbers than had been guessed, sending up placating but proud messages to the sun in continual ceremonies of dancing. The red percussion of their fires could be seen night and day by those waiting in the dark trance of the frozen town. Men were caught by the cold, they dropped in its snare-like silence. Bands of travelers moved closer together, with intenser caution, through the glassy tunnels of the Trace, for all proportion went away, and they followed one another like insects going at dawn through the heavy grass. Natchez people turned silently to look when a solitary man that no one had ever seen before was found and carried in through the streets, frozen the way he had crouched in a hollow tree, gray and huddled like a squirrel, with a little bundle of goods clasped to him.

Joel Mayes, a deaf boy twelve years old, saw the man brought in and knew it was a dead man, but his eyes were for something else, something wonderful. He saw the breaths coming out of people's mouths, and his dark face, losing just now a little of its softness, showed its secret desire. It was marvelous to him when the infinite designs of speech became visible in formations on the air, and he watched with awe that changed to tenderness whenever people met and passed in the road with an exchange of words. He walked alone, slowly through the silence, with the sturdy and yet dreamlike walk of the orphan, and let his own breath out through his lips, pushed it into the air, and whatever word it was it took the shape of a tower. He was as pleased as if he had had a little conversation with someone. At the end of the street, where he turned into the Inn, he always bent his head and walked faster, as if all frivolity were done, for he was boot-boy there.

He had come to Natchez some time in the summer. That was through great worlds of leaves, and the whole journey from Virginia had been to him a kind of childhood wandering in oblivion. He had remained to himself: always to himself at first,

and afterwards too—with the company of Old
Man McCaleb who took him along when his parents vanished in the forest, were cut off from him,
and in spite of his last backward look, dropped
behind. Arms bent on destination dragged him
forward through the sharp bushes, and leaves came
toward his face which he finally put his hands
out to stop. Now that he was a boot-boy, he had
thought little, frugally, almost stonily, of that
long time . . . until lately Old Man McCaleb
had reappeared at the Inn, bound for no telling
where, his tangled beard like the beards of old
men in dreams; and in the act of cleaning his
boots, which were uncommonly heavy and bur-
densome with mud, Joel came upon a little part
of the old adventure, for there it was, dark and
crusted . . . came back to it, and went over it
again. . . .

He rubbed, and remembered the day after his
parents had left him, the day when it was neces-
sary to hide from the Indians. Old Man McCaleb,
his stern face lighting in the most unexpected way,
had herded them, the whole party alike, into the
dense cane brake, deep down off the Trace—the
densest part, where it grew as thick and locked
as some kind of wild teeth. There they crouched,
and each one of them, man, woman, and child,
had looked at all the others from a hiding place
that seemed the least safe of all, watching in an

eager wild instinct for any movement or betrayal. Crouched by his bush, Joel had cried; all his understanding would desert him suddenly and because he could not hear he could not see or touch or find a familiar thing in the world. He wept, and Old Man McCaleb first felled the excited dog with the blunt end of his axe, and then he turned a fierce face toward him and lifted the blade in the air, in a kind of ecstasy of protecting the silence they were keeping. Joel had made a sound. . . . He gasped and put his mouth quicker than thought against the earth. He took the leaves in his mouth. . . . In that long time of lying motionless with the men and women in the cane brake he had learned what silence meant to other people. Through the danger he had felt acutely, even with horror, the nearness of his companions, a speechless embrace of which he had had no warning, a powerful, crushing unity. The Indians had then gone by, followed by an old woman— in solemn, single file, careless of the inflaming arrows they carried in their quivers, dangling in their hands a few strings of catfish. They passed in the length of the old woman's yawn. Then one by one McCaleb's charges had to rise up and come out of the hiding place. There was little talking together, but a kind of shame and shuffling. As soon as the party reached Natchez, their little cluster dissolved completely. The old man had given each of them one long, rather forlorn look for a farewell, and had gone away, no less preoccupied than he had ever been. To the man who had saved his life Joel lifted the gentle, almost indifferent face of the child who has asked for nothing. Now he remembered the white gulls flying across the sky behind the old man's head.

Joel had been deposited at the Inn, and there was nowhere else for him to go, for it stood there and marked the foot of the long Trace, with the river back of it. So he remained. It was a noncommittal arrangement: he never paid them anything for his keep, and they never paid him anything for his work. Yet time passed, and he became a little part of the place where it passed over him. A small private room became his own; it was on the ground floor behind the saloon, a dark little room paved with stones with its ceiling rafters curved not higher than a man's head. There was a fireplace and one window, which opened on the courtyard filled always with the tremor of horses. He curled up every night on a highbacked bench, when the weather turned cold he was given a collection of old coats to sleep under, and the room was almost excessively his own, as it would have been a stray kitten's that came to the same spot every night. He began to keep his candlestick carefully polished, he set it in the center of the puncheon table, and at night when it was lighted

all the messages of love carved into it with a knife
in Spanish words, with a deep Spanish gouging,
came out in black relief, for anyone to read who
came knowing the language.

Late at night, nearer morning, after the travelers had all certainly pulled off their boots to
fall into bed, he waked by habit and passed with
the candle shielded up the stairs and through
the halls and rooms, and gathered up the boots.
When he had brought them all down to his table
he would sit and take his own time cleaning them,
while the firelight would come gently across the
paving stones. It seemed then that his whole life
was safely alighted, in the sleep of everyone else,
like a bird on a bough, and he was alone in the
way he liked to be. He did not despise boots at all
—he had learned boots; under his hand they stood
up and took a good shape. This was not a slave's
work, or a child's either. It had dignity: it was
dangerous to walk about among sleeping men.
More than once he had been seized and the life
half shaken out of him by a man waking up in a
sweat of suspicion or nightmare, but he dealt
nimbly as an animal with the violence and quick
frenzy of dreamers. It might seem to him that the
whole world was sleeping in the lightest of trances,
which the least movement would surely wake;
but he only walked softly, stepping around and
over, and got back to his room. Once a rattlesnake

had shoved its head from a boot as he stretched out his hand; but that was not likely to happen again in a thousand years.

It was in his own room, on the night of the first snowfall, that a new adventure began for him. Very late in the night, toward morning, Joel sat bolt upright in bed and opened his eyes to see the whole room shining brightly, like a brimming lake in the sun. Boots went completely out of his head, and he was left motionless. The candle was lighted in its stick, the fire was high in the grate, and from the window a wild tossing illumination came, which he did not even identify at first as the falling of snow. Joel was left in the shadow of the room, and there before him, in the center of the strange multiplied light, were two men in black capes sitting at his table. They sat in profile to him, tall under the little arch of the rafters, facing each other across the good table he used for everything, and talking together. They were not of Natchez, and their names were not in the book. Each of them had a white glitter upon his boots— it was the snow; their capes were drawn together in front, and in the blackness of the folds, snowflakes were just beginning to melt.

Joel had never been able to hear the knocking at a door, and still he knew what that would be; and he surmised that these men had never knocked even lightly to enter his room. When he found that at some moment outside his knowledge or consent two men had seemingly fallen from the clouds onto the two stools at his table and had taken everything over for themselves, he did not keep the calm heart with which he had stood and regarded all men up to Old Man McCaleb, who snored upstairs.

He did not at once betray the violation that he felt. Instead, he simply sat, still bolt upright, and looked with the feasting the eyes do in secret—at their faces, the one eye of each that he could see, the cheeks, the half-hidden mouths—the faces each firelit, and strange with a common reminiscence or speculation. . . . Perhaps he was saved from giving a cry by knowing it could be heard. Then the gesture one of the men made in the air transfixed him where he waited.

One of the two men lifted his right arm—a tense, yet gentle and easy motion—and made the dark wet cloak fall back. To Joel it was like the first movement he had ever seen, as if the world had been up to that night inanimate. It was like the signal to open some heavy gate or paddock, and it did open to his complete astonishment upon a panorama in his own head, about which he knew first of all that he would never be able to speak—it was nothing but brightness, as full as the brightness on which he had opened his eyes. Inside his room was still another interior, this meeting upon which all the light was turned, and within that was one more mystery, all that was being said. The men's heads were inclined together against the blaze, their hair seemed light and floating. Their elbows rested on the boards, stirring the crumbs where Joel had eaten his biscuit. He had no idea of how long they had stayed when they got up and stretched their arms and walked out through the door, after blowing the candle out.

When Joel woke up again at daylight, his first thought was of Indians, his next of ghosts, and then the vision of what had happened came back into his head. He took a light beating for forgetting to clean the boots, but then he forgot the beating. He wondered for how long a time the men had been meeting in his room while he was asleep, and whether they had ever seen him, and what they might be going to do to him, whether they would take him each by the arm and drag him on further, through the leaves. He tried to remember everything of the night before, and he could, and then of the day before, and he rubbed belatedly at a boot in a long and deepening dream. His memory could work like the slinging of a noose to catch a wild pony. It reached back and hung trembling over the very moment of terror in which he had become separated from his parents, and then it turned and started in the oppo-

site direction, and it would have discerned some
shape, but he would not let it, of the future. In
the meanwhile, all day long, everything in the
passing moment and each little deed assumed the
gravest importance. He divined every change in
the house, in the angle of the doors, in the height
of the fires, and whether the logs had been stirred
by a boot or had only fallen in an empty room.
He was seized and possessed by mystery. He waited
for night. In his own room the candlestick now
stood on the table covered with the wonder of
having been touched by unknown hands in his
absence and seen in his sleep.

It was while he was cleaning boots again that
the identity of the men came to him all at once.
Like part of his meditations, the names came into
his mind. He ran out into the street with this
knowledge rocking in his head, remembering then
the tremor of a great arrival which had shaken
Natchez, caught fast in the grip of the cold, and
shaken it through the lethargy of the snow, and
it was clear now why the floors swayed with running feet and unsteady hands shoved him aside at
the bar. There was no one to inform him that the
men were Aaron Burr and Harman Blennerhassett, but he knew. No one had pointed out to him
any way that he might know which was which, but
he knew that: it was Burr who had made the gesture.

They came to his room every night, and indeed Joel had not expected that the one visit would be the end. It never occurred to him that the first meeting did not mark a beginning. It took a little time always for the snow to melt from their capes —for it continued all this time to snow. Joel sat up with his eyes wide open in the shadows and looked out like the lone watcher of a conflagration. The room grew warm, burning with the heat from the little grate, but there was something of fire in all that happened. It was from Aaron Burr that the flame was springing, and it seemed to pass across the table with certain words and through the sudden nobleness of the gesture, and touch Blennerhassett. Yet the breath of their speech was no simple thing like the candle's gleam between them. Joel saw them still only in profile, but he could see that the secret was endlessly complex, for in two nights it was apparent that it could never be all told. All that they said never finished their conversation. They would always have to meet again. The ring Burr wore caught the firelight repeatedly and started it up again in the intricate whirlpool of a signet. Quicker and fuller still was his eye, darting its look about, but never at Joel. Their eyes had never really seen his room . . . the fine polish he had given the candlestick, the clean boards from which he had scraped the crumbs, the wooden bench where he was himself, from which he put outward—just a little, carelessly—his hand. . . . Everything in the room was conquest, all was a dream of delights and powers beyond its walls. . . . The light-filled hair fell over Burr's sharp forehead, his cheek grew taut, his smile was sudden, his lips drove the breath through. The other man's face, with its quiet mouth, for he was the listener, changed from ardor to gloom and back to ardor. . . . Joel sat still and looked from one man to the other.

At first he believed that he had not been discovered. Then he knew that they had learned somehow of his presence, and that it had not stopped them. Somehow that appalled him. . . . They were aware that if it were only before him, they could talk forever in his room. Then he put it that they accepted him. One night, in his first realization of this, his defect seemed to him a kind of hospitality. A joy came over him, he was moved to gaiety, he felt wit stirring in his mind, and he came out of his hiding place and took a few steps toward them. Finally, it was too much: he broke in upon the circle of their talk, and set food and drink from the kitchen on the table between them. His hands were shaking, and they looked at him as if from great distances, but they were not surprised, and he could smell the familiar black wetness of travelers' clothes steaming up from them in the firelight. Afterwards he sat on the floor perfectly still, with Burr's cloak hanging just beside his own shoulder. At such moments he felt a dizziness as if the cape swung him about in a great arc of wonder, but Aaron Burr turned his full face and looked down at him only with gravity, the high margin of his brows lifted above tireless eyes.

There was a kind of dominion promised in his gentlest glance. When he first would come and throw himself down to talk and the fire would flame up and the reflections of the snowy world grew bright, even the clumsy table seemed to change its substance and to become a part of a ceremony. He might have talked in another language, in which there was nothing but evocation. When he was seen so plainly, all his movements and his looks seemed part of a devotion that was curiously patient and had the illusion of wisdom all about it. Lights shone in his eyes like travelers' fires seen far out on the river. Always he talked, his talking was his appearance, as if there were no eyes, nose, or mouth to remember; in his face there was every subtlety and eloquence, and no features, no kindness, for there was no awareness whatever of the present. Looking up from the floor at his speaking face, Joel knew all at once some secret of temptation and an anguish that would reach out after it like a closing hand. He would allow Burr to take him with him wherever it was that he meant to go.

Sometimes in the nights Joel would feel himself surely under their eyes, and think they must have come; but that would be a dream, and when he sat up on his bench he often saw nothing more than the dormant firelight stretched on the empty floor, and he would have a strange feeling of having been deserted and lost, not quite like anything he had ever felt in his life. It was likely to be early dawn before they came.

When they were there, he sat restored, though they paid no more attention to him than they paid the presence of the firelight. He brought all the food he could manage to give them; he saved a little out of his own suppers, and one night he stole a turkey pie. He might have been their safety, for the way he sat up so still and looked at them at moments like a father at his playing children. He never for an instant wished for them to leave, though he would so long for sleep that he would stare at them finally in bewilderment and without a single flicker of the eyelid. Often they would talk all night. Blennerhassett's wide vague face would grow out of devotion into exhaustion. But Burr's hand would always reach across and take him by the shoulder as if to rouse him from a dull sleep, and the radiance of his own face would heighten always with the passing of time. Joel sat quietly, waiting for the full revelation of the meetings. All his love went out to the talkers. He would not have known how to hold it back.

In the idle mornings, in some morning need to go looking at the world, he wandered down to the Esplanade and stood under the trees which bent heavily over his head. He frowned out across the ice-covered racetrack and out upon the river. There was one hour when the river was the color of smoke, as if it were more a thing of the woods than an element and a power in itself. It seemed to belong to the woods, to be gentle and watched over, a tethered and grazing pet of the forest, and then when the light spread higher and color stained the world, the river would leap suddenly out of the shining ice around, into its full-grown torrent of life, and its strength and its churning passage held Joel watching over it like the spell unfolding by night in his room. If he could not speak to the river, and he could not, still he would try to read in the river's blue and violet skeins a working of the momentous event. It was hard to understand. Was any scheme a man had, however secret and intact, always broken upon by the very current of its working? One day, in anguish, he saw a raft torn apart in midstream and the men scattered from it. Then all that he felt move in his heart at the sight of the inscrutable river went out in hope for the two men and their genius that he sheltered.

It was when he returned to the Inn that he was given a notice to paste on the saloon mirror saying that the trial of Aaron Burr for treason would be held at the end of the month at Washington, capitol of Mississippi Territory, on the campus of Jefferson College, where the crowds might be amply accommodated. In the meanwhile, the arrival of the full, armed flotilla was being awaited, and the price of whisky would not be advanced in this tavern, but there would be a slight increase in the tariff on a bed upstairs, depending on how many slept in it.

The month wore on, and now it was full moonlight. Late at night the whole sky was lunar, like the surface of the moon brought as close as a cheek. The luminous ranges of all the clouds stretched one beyond the other in heavenly order. They seemed to be the streets where Joel was walking through the town. People now lighted their houses in entertainments as if they copied after the sky, with Burr in the center of them always, dancing with the women, talking with the men. They followed and formed cotillion figures about the one who threatened or lured them, and their minuets skimmed across the nights like a pebble expertly skipped across water. Joel would watch them take sides, and watch the arguments, all the frilled motions and the toasts, and he thought they were to decide whether Burr was good or evil. But all the time, Joel believed, when he saw Burr go dancing by, that did not touch him at all. Joel knew his eyes saw nothing there and went always beyond the room, although usually the most beautiful woman there was somehow in his arms when the set was over. Sometimes they drove him in their carriages down to the Esplanade and pointed out the moon to him, to end the evening. There they sat showing everything to Aaron Burr, nodding with a magnificence that approached fatigue toward the reaches of the ice that stretched over the river like an impossible bridge, some extension to the West of the Natchez Trace; and a radiance as soft and near as rain fell on their hands and faces, and on the plumes of the breaths from the horses' nostrils, and they were as gracious and as grand as Burr.

Each day that drew the trial closer, men talked more hotly on the corners and the saloon at the Inn shook with debate; every night Burr was invited to a finer and later ball; and Joel waited. He knew that Burr was being allotted, by an almost specific consent, this free and unmolested time till dawn, to meet in conspiracy, for the sake of continuing and perfecting the secret. This knowledge Joel gathered to himself by being, himself, everywhere; it decreed his own suffering and made it secret and filled with private omens.

One day he was driven to know everything. It was the morning he was given a little fur cap, and he set it on his head and started out. He walked through the dark trodden snow all the way up the

Trace to the Bayou Pierre. The great trees began to break that day. The pounding of their explosions filled the subdued air; to Joel it was as if a great foot had stamped on the ground. And at first he thought he saw the fulfillment of all the rumor and promise—the flotilla coming around the bend, and he did not know whether he felt terror or pride. But then he saw that what covered the river over was a chain of great perfect trees floating down, lying on their sides in postures like slain giants and heroes of battle, black cedars and stone-white sycamores, magnolias with their leavy leaves shining as if they were in bloom, a long procession. Then it was terror that he felt.

He went on. He was not the only one who had made the pilgrimage to see what the original flotilla was like, that had been taken from Burr. There were many others: there was Old Man McCaleb, at a little distance. . . . In care not to show any excitement of expectation, Joel made his way through successive little groups that seemed to meditate there above the encampment of militia on the snowy bluff, and looked down at the water.

There was no galley there. There were nine small flatboats tied to the shore. They seemed so small and delicate that he was shocked and distressed, and looked around at the faces of the others, who looked coolly back at him. There was no sign of weapon about the boats or anywhere, except in the hands of the men on guard. There were barrels of molasses and whisky, rolling and knocking each other like drowned men, and stowed to one side of one of the boats, in a dark place, a strange little collection of blankets, a silver bridle with bells, a book swollen with water, and a little flute with a narrow ridge of snow along it. Where Joel stood looking down upon them, the boats floated in clusters of three, as small as water-lilies on a still bayou. A canoe filled with crazily wrapped-up Indians passed at a little distance, and with severe open mouths the Indians all laughed.

But the soldiers were sullen with cold, and very grave or angry, and Old Man McCaleb was there with his beard flying and his finger pointing prophetically in the direction of upstream. Some of the soldiers and all the women nodded their heads, as though they were the easiest believers, and one woman drew her child tightly to her. Joel shivered. Two of the young men hanging over the edge of the bluff flung their arms in sudden exhilaration about each other's shoulders, and a look of wildness came over their faces.

Back in the streets of Natchez, Joel met part of the militia marching and stood with his heart racing, back out of the way of the line coming with bright guns tilted up in the sharp air. Behind

them, two of the soldiers dragged along a young
dandy whose eyes glared at everything. There
where they held him he was trying over and over
again to make Aaron Burr's gesture, and he never
convinced anybody.

Joel went in all three times to the militia's encampment on the Bayou Pierre, the last time on
the day before the trial was to begin. Then out beyond a willow point a rowboat with one soldier
in it kept laconic watch upon the north.

Joel returned on the frozen path to the Inn,
and stumbled into his room, and waited for Burr
and Blennerhassett to come and talk together. His
head ached. . . . All his walking about was no
use. Where did people learn things? Where did
they go to find them? How far?

Burr and Blennerhassett talked across the table,
and it was growing late on the last night. Then
there in the doorway with a fiddle in her hand
stood Blennerhassett's wife, wearing breeches,
come to fetch him home. The fiddle she had
simply picked up in the Inn parlor as she came
through, and Joel did not think she bothered
now to speak at all. But she waited there before
the fire, still a child and so clearly related to her
husband that their sudden movements at the encounter were alike and made at the same time.
They stood looking at each other there in the

firelight like creatures balancing together on a raft, and then she lifted the bow and began to play.

Joel gazed at the girl, not much older than himself. She leaned her cheek against the fiddle. He had never examined a fiddle at all, and when she began to play it she frightened and dismayed him by her almost insect-like motions, the pensive antennae of her arms, her mask of a countenance. When she played she never blinked her eye. Her legs, fantastic in breeches, were separated slightly, and from her bent knees she swayed back and forth as if she were weaving the tunes with her body. The sharp odor of whisky moved with her. The slits of her eyes were milky. The songs she played seemed to him to have no beginnings and no endings, but to be about many hills and valleys, and chains of lakes. She, like the men, knew of a place. . . . All of them spoke of a country.

And quite clearly, and altogether to his surprise, Joel saw a sight that he had nearly forgotten. Instead of the fire on the hearth, there was a mimosa tree in flower. It was in the little back field at his home in Virginia and his mother was leading him by the hand. Fragile, delicate, cloudlike it rose on its pale trunk and spread its long level arms. His mother pointed to it. Among the trembling leaves the feathery puffs of sweet bloom filled the tree like thousands of paradisical birds all alighted at an instant. He had known then the story of the Princess Labam, for his mother had told it to him, how she was so radiant that she sat on the roof-top at night and lighted the city. It seemed to be the mimosa tree that lighted the garden, for its brightness and fragrance overlaid all the rest. Out of its graciousness this tree suffered their presence and shed its splendor upon him and his mother. His mother pointed again, and its scent swayed like the Asiatic princess moving up and down the pink steps of its branches. Then the vision was gone. Aaron Burr sat in front of the fire, Blennerhassett faced him, and Blennerhassett's wife played on the violin.

There was no compassion in what this woman was doing, he knew that—there was only a frightening thing, a stern allurement. Try as he might, he could not comprehend it, though it was so calculated. He had instead a sensation of pain, the ends of his fingers were stinging. At first he did not realize that he had heard the sounds of her song, the only thing he had ever heard. Then all at once as she held the lifted bow still for a moment he gasped for breath at the interruption, and he did not care to learn her purpose or to wonder any longer, but bent his head and listened for the note that she would fling down upon them. And it was so gentle then, it touched him with surprise; it made him think of animals sleeping on their cushioned paws.

For a moment his love went like sound into a myriad life and was divided among all the people in his room. While they listened, Burr's radiance was somehow quenched, or theirs was raised to equal it, and they were all alike. There was one thing that shone in all their faces, and that was how far they were from home, how far from everywhere that they knew. Joel put his hand to his own face, and hid his pity from them while they listened to the endless tunes.

But she ended them. Sleep all at once seemed to overcome her whole body. She put down the fiddle and took Blennerhassett by both hands. He seemed tired too, more tired than talking could ever make him. He went out when she led him. They went wrapped under one cloak, his arm about her.

Burr did not go away immediately. First he walked up and down before the fire. He turned each time with diminishing violence, and light and shadow seemed to stream more softly with his turning cloak. Then he stood still. The firelight threw its changes over his face. He had no one to talk to. His boots smelled of the fire's closeness. Of course he had forgotten Joel, he seemed quite alone. At last with a strange naturalness, almost with a limp, he went to the table and stretched himself full length upon it.

He lay on his back. Joel was astonished. That

was the way they laid out the men killed in duels
in the Inn yard; and that was the table they laid
them on.

Burr fell asleep instantly, so quickly that Joel
felt he should never be left alone. He looked at
the sleeping face of Burr, and the time and the
place left him, and all that Burr had said that he
had tried to guess left him too—he knew nothing
in the world except the sleeping face. It was quiet.
The eyes were almost closed, only dark slits lay
beneath the lids. There was a small scar on the
cheek. The lips were parted. Joel thought, I could
speak if I would, or I could hear. Once I did each
thing. . . . Still he listened . . . and it seemed
that all that would speak, in this world, was listening. Burr was silent; he demanded nothing, nothing. . . . A boy or a man could be so alone in his
heart that he could not even ask a question. In
such silence as falls over a lonely man there is
childlike supplication, and all arms might wish to
open to him, but there is no speech. This was
Burr's last night: Joel knew that. This was the
moment before he would ride away. Why would
the heart break so at absence? Joel knew that it
was because nothing had been told. The heart is
secret even when the moment it dreamed of has
come, a moment when there might have been a
revelation. . . . Joel stood motionless; he lifted
his gaze from Burr's face and stared at nothing.

. . . If love does a secret thing always, it is to reach backward, to a time that could not be known —for it makes a history of the sorrow and the dream it has contemplated in some instant of recognition. What Joel saw before him he had a terrible wish to speak out loud, but he would have had to find names for the places of the heart and the times for its shadowy and tragic events, and they seemed of great magnitude, heroic and terrible and splendid, like the legends of the mind. But for lack of a way to tell how much was known, the boundaries would lie between him and the others, all the others, until he died.

Presently Burr began to toss his head and to cry out. He talked, his face drew into a dreadful set of grimaces, which it followed over and over. He could never stop talking. Joel was afraid of these words, and afraid that eavesdroppers might listen to them. Whatever words they were, they were being taken by some force out of his dream. In horror, Joel put out his hand. He could never in his life have laid it across the mouth of Aaron Burr, but he thrust it into Burr's spread-out fingers. The fingers closed and did not yield; the clasp grew so fierce that it hurt his hand, but he saw that the words had stopped.

As if a silent love had shown him whatever new thing he would ever be able to learn, Joel had some wisdom in his fingers now which only this

long month could have brought. He knew with
what gentleness to hold the burning hand. With
the gravity of his very soul he received the furious
pressure of this man's dream. At last Burr drew
his arm back beside his quiet head, and his hand
hung like a child's in sleep, released in oblivion.

The next morning, Joel was given a notice to
paste on the saloon mirror that conveyances might
be rented at the Inn daily for the excursion to
Washington for the trial of Mr. Burr, payment to
be made in advance. Joel went out and stood on a
corner, and joined with a group of young boys
walking behind the militia.

It was warm—a "false spring" day. The little
procession from Natchez, decorated and smiling
in all they owned or whatever they borrowed or
chartered or rented, moved grandly through the
streets and on up the Trace. To Joel, somewhere
in the line, the blue air that seemed to lie between
the high banks held it all in a mist, softly colored,
the fringe waving from a carriage top, a few flags
waving, a sword shining when some gentleman
made a flourish. High up on their horses a number of the men were wearing their Revolutionary
War uniforms, as if to reiterate that Aaron Burr
fought once at their sides as a hero.

Under the spreading live-oaks at Washington,
the trial opened like a festival. There was a theatre

of benches, and a promenade; stalls were set out under the trees and glasses of whisky, and colored ribbons, were sold. Joel sat somewhere among the crowds. Breezes touched the yellow and violet of dresses and stirred them, horses pawed the ground, and the people pressed upon him and seemed more real than those in dreams, and yet their pantomime was like those choruses and companies whose movements are like the waves running together. A hammer was then pounded, there was sudden attention from all the spectators, and Joel felt the great solidifying of their silence.

He had dreaded the sight of Burr. He had thought there might be some mark or disfigurement that would come from his panic. But all his grace was back upon him, and he was smiling to greet the studious faces which regarded him. Before their bright façade others rose first, declaiming men in turn, and then Burr.

In a moment he was walking up and down with his shadow on the grass and the patches of snow. He was talking again, talking now in great courtesy to everybody. There was a flickering light of sun and shadow on his face.

Then Joel understood. Burr was explaining away, smoothing over all that he had held great enough to have dreaded once. He walked back and forth elegantly in the sun, turning his wrist ever so airily in its frill, making light of his dream that

had terrified him. And it was the deed they had all
come to see. All around Joel they gasped, smiled,
pressed one another's arms, nodded their heads;
there were tender smiles on the women's faces.
They were at Aaron Burr's feet at last, learning
their superiority. They loved him now, in their
condescension. They leaned forward in delight at
the parading spectacle he was making. And when
it was over for the day, they shook each other's
hands, and Old Man McCaleb could be seen spit-
ting on the ground, in the anticipation of another
day as good as this one.

Blennerhassett did not come that night.

Burr came very late. He walked in the door,
looked down at Joel where he sat among his boots,
and suddenly stooped and took the dirty cloth out
of his hand. He put his face quickly into it and
pressed and rubbed it against his skin. Joel saw
that all his clothes were dirty and ragged. The last
thing he did was to set a little cap of turkey feathers on his head. Then he went out.

Joel followed him along behind the dark houses
and through a ravine. Burr turned toward the
Halfway Hill. Joel turned too, and he saw Burr
walk slowly up and open the great heavy gate.

He saw him stop beside a tall camellia bush as
solid as a tower and pick up one of the frozen
buds which were shed all around it on the ground.

For a moment he held it in the palm of his hand, and then he went on. Joel, following behind, did the same. He held the bud, and studied the burned edges of its folds by the pale half-light of the East. The bud came apart in his hand, its layers like small velvet shells, still iridescent, the shriveled flower inside. He held it tenderly and yet timidly, in a kind of shame, as though all disaster lay pitifully disclosed now to the eyes.

He knew the girl Burr had often danced with under the rings of tapers when she came out in a cloak across the shadowy hill. Burr stood, quiet and graceful as he had always been as her partner at the balls. Joel felt a pain like a sting while she first merged with the dark figure and then drew back. The moon, late-risen and waning, came out of the clouds. Aaron Burr made the gesture there in the distance, toward the West, where the clouds hung still and red, and when Joel looked at him in the light he saw as she must have seen the absurdity he was dressed in, the feathers on his head. With a curious feeling of revenge upon her, he watched her turn, draw smaller within her own cape, and go away.

Burr came walking down the hill, and passed close to the camellia bush where Joel was standing. He walked stiffly in his mock Indian dress with the boot polish on his face. The youngest child in Natchez would have known that this was a remarkable and wonderful figure that had humiliated itself by disguise.

Pausing in an open space, Burr lifted his hand once more and a slave led out from the shadows a majestic horse with silver trappings shining in the light of the moon. Burr mounted from the slave's hand in all the clarity of his true elegance, and sat for a moment motionless in the saddle. Then he cut his whip through the air, and rode away.

Joel followed him on foot toward the Liberty Road. As he walked through the streets of Natchez he felt a strange mourning to know that Burr would never come again by that way. If he had left in disguise, the thirst that was in his face was the same as it had ever been. He had eluded judgment, that was all he had done, and Joel was glad while he still trembled. Joel would never know now the true course, or the true outcome of any dream: this was all he felt. But he walked on, in the frozen path into the wilderness, on and on. He did not see how he could ever go back and still be the boot-boy at the Inn.

He did not know how far he had gone on the Liberty Road when the posse came riding up behind and passed him. He walked on. He saw that the bodies of the frozen birds had fallen out of the trees, and he fell down and wept for his father and mother, to whom he had not said goodbye.

THE WIDE NET

This Story is For
JOHN FRAISER ROBINSON

*W*ILLIAM WALLACE JAMIESON'S
wife Hazel was going to have a baby. But this was
October, and it was six months away, and she
acted exactly as though it would be tomorrow.
When he came in the room she would not speak
to him, but would look as straight at nothing as
she could, with her eyes glowing. If he only
touched her she stuck out her tongue or ran
around the table. So one night he went out with
two of the boys down the road and stayed out all
night. But that was the worst thing yet, because
when he came home in the early morning Hazel
had vanished. He went through the house not believing his eyes, balancing with both hands out,
his yellow cowlick rising on end, and then he
turned the kitchen inside out looking for her, but
it did no good. Then when he got back to the

34

front room he saw she had left him a little letter,
in an envelope. That was doing something behind
someone's back. He took out the letter, pushed
it open, held it out at a distance from his eyes.
. . . After one look he was scared to read the exact words, and he crushed the whole thing in his
hand instantly, but what it had said was that she
would not put up with him after that and was
going to the river to drown herself.

"Drown herself. . . . But she's in mortal fear
of the water!"

He ran out front, his face red like the red of the
picked cotton field he ran over, and down in the
road he gave a loud shout for Virgil Thomas, who
was just going in his own house, to come out again.
He could just see the edge of Virgil, he had almost got in, he had one foot inside the door.

They met half-way between the farms, under
the shade-tree.

"Haven't you had enough of the night?" asked
Virgil. There they were, their pants all covered
with dust and dew, and they had had to carry the
third man home flat between them.

"I've lost Hazel, she's vanished, she went to
drown herself."

"Why, that ain't like Hazel," said Virgil.

William Wallace reached out and shook him.
"You heard me. Don't you know we have to drag
the river?"

"Right this minute?"

"You ain't got nothing to do till spring."

"Let me go set foot inside the house and speak to my mother and tell her a story, and I'll come back."

"This will take the wide net," said William Wallace. His eyebrows gathered, and he was talking to himself.

"How come Hazel to go and do that way?" asked Virgil as they started out.

William Wallace said, "I reckon she got lonesome."

"That don't argue—drown herself for getting lonesome. My mother gets lonesome."

"Well," said William Wallace. "It argues for Hazel."

"How long is it now since you and her was married?"

"Why, it's been a year."

"It don't seem that long to me. A year!"

"It was this time last year. It seems longer," said William Wallace, breaking a stick off a tree in surprise. They walked along, kicking at the flowers on the road's edge. "I remember the day I seen her first, and that seems a long time ago. She was coming along the road holding a little frying-size chicken from her grandma, under her arm, and she had it real quiet. I spoke to her with nice

manners. We knowed each other's names, being
bound to, just didn't know each other to speak to.
I says, 'Where are you taking the fryer?' and she
says, 'Mind your manners,' and I kept on till after
while she says, 'If you want to walk me home, take
littler steps.' So I didn't lose time. It was just four
miles across the field and full of blackberries, and
from the top of the hill there was Dover below,
looking sizeable-like and clean, spread out between the two churches like that. When we got
down, I says to her, 'What kind of water's in this
well?' and she says, 'The best water in the world.'
So I drew a bucket and took out a dipper and she
drank and I drank. I didn't think it was that remarkable, but I didn't tell her."

"What happened that night?" asked Virgil.

"We ate the chicken," said William Wallace,
"and it was tender. Of course that wasn't all they
had. The night I was trying their table out, it
sure had good things to eat from one end to the
other. Her mama and papa sat at the head and
foot and we was face to face with each other across
it, with I remember a pat of butter between. They
had real sweet butter, with a tree drawed down it,
elegant-like. Her mama eats like a man. I had
brought her a whole hat-ful of berries and she
didn't even pass them to her husband. Hazel, she
would leap up and take a pitcher of new milk and
fill up the glasses. I had heard how they couldn't

have a singing at the church without a fight over her."

"Oh, she's a pretty girl, all right," said Virgil. "It's a pity for the ones like her to grow old, and get like their mothers."

"Another thing will be that her mother will get wind of this and come after me," said William Wallace.

"Her mother will eat you alive," said Virgil.

"She's just been watching her chance," said William Wallace. "Why did I think I could stay out all night."

"Just something come over you."

"First it was just a carnival at Carthage, and I had to let them guess my weight . . . and after that . . ."

"It was nice to be sitting on your neck in a ditch singing," prompted Virgil, "in the moonlight. And playing on the harmonica like you can play."

"Even if Hazel did sit home knowing I was drunk, that wouldn't kill her," said William Wallace. "What she knows ain't ever killed her yet. . . . She's smart, too, for a girl," he said.

"She's a lot smarter than her cousins in Beula," said Virgil. "And especially Edna Earle, that never did get to be what you'd call a heavy thinker. Edna Earle could sit and ponder all day on how the little tail of the 'C' got through the 'L' in a Coca-Cola sign."

"Hazel *is* smart," said William Wallace. They walked on. "You ought to see her pantry shelf, it looks like a hundred jars when you open the door. I don't see how she could turn around and jump in the river."

"It's a woman's trick."

"I always behaved before. Till the one night— last night."

"Yes, but the one night," said Virgil. "And she was waiting to take advantage."

"She jumped in the river because she was scared to death of the water and that was to make it worse," he said. "She remembered how I used to have to pick her up and carry her over the oak-log bridge, how she'd shut her eyes and make a dead-weight and hold me round the neck, just for a little creek. I don't see how she brought herself to jump."

"Jumped backwards," said Virgil. "Didn't look."

When they turned off, it was still early in the pink and green fields. The fumes of morning, sweet and bitter, sprang up where they walked. The insects ticked softly, their strength in reserve; butterflies chopped the air, going to the east, and the birds flew carelessly and sang by fits

and starts, not the way they did in the evening in
sustained and drowsy songs.

"It's a pretty *day* for sure," said William Wallace. "It's a pretty *day* for it."

"I don't see a sign of her ever going along here,"
said Virgil.

"Well," said William Wallace. "She wouldn't
have dropped anything. I never saw a girl to leave
less signs of where she's been."

"Not even a plum seed," said Virgil, kicking
the grass.

In the grove it was so quiet that once William
Wallace gave a jump, as if he could almost hear
a sound of himself wondering where she had gone.
A descent of energy came down on him in the
thick of the woods and he ran at a rabbit and
caught it in his hands.

"Rabbit . . . Rabbit . . ." He acted as if he
wanted to take it off to himself and hold it up and
talk to it. He laid a palm against its pushing heart.
"Now . . . There now . . ."

"Let her go, William Wallace, let her go."
Virgil, chewing on an elderberry whistle he had
just made, stood at his shoulder: "What do you
want with a live rabbit?"

William Wallace squatted down and set the rabbit on the ground but held it under his hand. It
was a little, old, brown rabbit. It did not try to
move. "See there?"

"Let her go."

"She can go if she wants to, but she don't want to."

Gently he lifted his hand. The round eye was shining at him sideways in the green gloom.

"Anybody can freeze a rabbit, that wants to," said Virgil. Suddenly he gave a far-reaching blast on the whistle, and the rabbit went in a streak. "Was you out catching cotton-tails, or was you out catching your wife?" he said, taking the turn to the open fields. "I come along to keep you on the track."

"Who'll we get, now?" They stood on top of a hill and William Wallace looked critically over the countryside. "Any of the Malones?"

"I was always scared of the Malones," said Virgil. "Too many *of* them."

"This is my day with the net, and they would have to watch out," said William Wallace. "I reckon some Malones, and the Doyles, will be enough. The six Doyles and their dogs, and you and me, and two little nigger boys is enough, with just a few Malones."

"That ought to be enough," said Virgil, "no matter what."

"I'll bring the Malones, and you bring the Doyles," said William Wallace, and they separated at the spring.

When William Wallace came back, with a string of Malones just showing behind him on the hilltop, he found Virgil with the two little Rippen boys waiting behind him, solemn little towheads. As soon as he walked up, Grady, the one in front, lifted his hand to signal silence and caution to his brother Brucie who began panting merrily and untrustworthily behind him.

Brucie bent readily under William Wallace's hand-pat, and gave him a dreamy look out of the tops of his round eyes, which were pure green-and-white like clover tops. William Wallace gave him a nickel. Grady hung his head; his white hair lay in a little tail in the nape of his neck.

"Let's let them come," said Virgil.

"Well, they can come then, but if we keep letting everybody come it is going to be too many," said William Wallace.

"They'll appreciate it, those little-old boys," said Virgil. Brucie held up at arm's length a long red thread with a bent pin tied on the end; and a look of helpless and intense interest gathered Grady's face like a drawstring—his eyes, one bright with a sty, shone pleadingly under his white bangs, and he snapped his jaw and tried to speak. . . . "Their papa was drowned in the Pearl River," said Virgil.

There was a shout from the gully.

"Here come all the Malones," cried William

Wallace. "I asked four of them would they come, but the rest of the family invited themselves."

"Did you ever see a time when they didn't," said Virgil. "And yonder from the other direction comes the Doyles, still with biscuit crumbs on their cheeks, I bet, now it's nothing to do but eat as their mother said."

"If two little niggers would come along now, or one big nigger," said William Wallace. And the words were hardly out of his mouth when two little Negro boys came along, going somewhere, one behind the other, stepping high and gay in their overalls, as though they waded in honeydew to the waist.

"Come here, boys. What's your names?"

"Sam and Robbie Bell."

"Come along with us, we're going to drag the river."

"You hear that, Robbie Bell?" said Sam.

They smiled.

The Doyles came noiselessly, their dogs made all the fuss. The Malones, eight giants with great long black eyelashes, were already stamping the ground and pawing each other, ready to go. Everybody went up together to see Doc.

Old Doc owned the wide net. He had a house on top of the hill and he sat and looked out from a rocker on the front porch.

✦

"Climb the hill and come in!" he began to intone across the valley. "Harvest's over . . . slipped up on everybody . . . cotton's picked, gone to the gin . . . hay cut . . . molasses made around here. . . . Big explosion's over, super-visors elected, some pleased, some not. . . . We're hearing talk of war!"

When they got closer, he was saying, "Many's been saved at revival, twenty-two last Sunday including a Doyle, ought to counted two. Hope they'll be a blessing to Dover community besides a shining star in Heaven. Now what?" he asked, for they had arrived and stood gathered in front of the steps.

"If nobody is using your wide net, could we use it?" asked William Wallace.

"You just used it a month ago," said Doc. "It ain't your turn."

Virgil jogged William Wallace's arm and cleared his throat. "This time is kind of special," he said. "We got reason to think William Wallace's wife Hazel is in the river, drowned."

"What reason have you got to think she's in the river drowned?" asked Doc. He took out his old pipe "I'm asking the husband."

"Because she's not in the house," said William Wallace.

"Vanished?" and he knocked out the pipe.

"Plum vanished."

"Of course a thousand things could have happened to her," said Doc, and he lighted the pipe.

"Hand him up the letter, William Wallace," said Virgil. "We can't wait around till Doomsday for the net while Doc sits back thinkin'."

"I tore it up, right at the first," said William Wallace. "But I know it by heart. It said she was going to jump straight in the Pearl River and that I'd be sorry."

"Where do you come in, Virgil?" asked Doc.

"I was in the same place William Wallace sat on his neck in, all night, and done as much as he done, and come home the same time."

"You-all were out cuttin' up, so Lady Hazel has to jump in the river, is that it? Cause and effect? Anybody want to argue with me? Where do these others come in, Doyles, Malones, and what not?"

"Doc is the smartest man around," said William Wallace, turning to the solidly waiting Doyles, "but it sure takes time."

"These are the ones that's collected to drag the river for her," said Virgil.

"Of course I am not going on record to say so soon that *I* think she's drowned," Doc said, blowing out blue smoke.

"Do you think . . ." William Wallace mounted a step, and his hands both went into fists. "Do you think she was *carried off*?"

"Now that's the way to argue, see it from all sides," said Doc promptly. "But who by?"

Some Malone whistled, but not so you could tell which one.

"There's no booger around the Dover section that goes around carrying off young girls that's married," stated Doc.

"She was always scared of the Gypsies." William Wallace turned scarlet. "She'd sure turn her ring around on her finger if she passed one, and look in the other direction so they couldn't see she was pretty and carry her off. They come in the end of summer."

"Yes, there are the Gypsies, kidnappers since the world began. But was it to be you that would pay the grand ransom?" asked Doc. He pointed his finger. They all laughed then at how clever old Doc was and clapped William Wallace on the back. But that turned into a scuffle and they fell to the ground.

"Stop it, or you can't have the net," said Doc. "You're scaring my wife's chickens."

"It's time we was gone," said William Wallace.

The big barking dogs jumped to lean their front paws on the men's chests.

"My advice remains, Let well enough alone," said Doc. "Whatever this mysterious event will turn out to be, it has kept one woman from talking a while. However, Lady Hazel is the prettiest girl in Mississippi, you've never seen a prettier one and you never will. A golden-haired girl." He got to his feet with the nimbleness that was always his surprise, and said, "I'll come along with you."

The path they always followed was the Old Natchez Trace. It took them through the deep woods and led them out down below on the Pearl River, where they could begin dragging it upstream to a point near Dover. They walked in silence around William Wallace, not letting him carry anything, but the net dragged heavily and the buckets were full of clatter in a place so dim and still.

Once they went through a forest of cucumber trees and came up on a high ridge. Grady and Brucie who were running ahead all the way stopped in their tracks; a whistle had blown and far down and far away a long freight train was passing. It seemed like a little festival procession, moving with the slowness of ignorance or a dream, from distance to distance, the tiny pink and gray cars like secret boxes. Grady was counting the cars to himself, as if he could certainly see each one clearly, and Brucie watched his lips, hushed and cautious, the way he would watch a bird drinking. Tears suddenly came to Grady's eyes, but it could only be because a tiny man walked along the top of the train, walking and moving on top of the moving train.

They went down again and soon the smell of the river spread over the woods, cool and secret. Every step they took among the great walls of vines and among the passion-flowers started up a little life, a little flight.

"We're walking along in the changing-time," said Doc. "Any day now the change will come. It's going to turn from hot to cold, and we can kill the hog that's ripe and have fresh meat to eat. Come one of these nights and we can wander down here and tree a nice possum. Old Jack Frost will be pinching things up. Old Mr. Winter will be standing in the door. Hickory tree there will be yellow. Sweet-gum red, hickory yellow, dogwood red, sycamore yellow." He went along rapping the tree trunks with his knuckle. "Magnolia and live-oak never die. Remember that. Persimmons will all get fit to eat, and the nuts will be dropping like rain all through the woods here. And run, little quail, run, for we'll be after you too."

They went on and suddenly the woods opened upon light, and they had reached the river. Every-one stopped, but Doc talked on ahead as though nothing had happened. "Only today," he said, "to-day, in October sun, it's all gold—sky and tree and water. Everything just before it changes looks to be made of gold."

William Wallace looked down, as though he thought of Hazel with the shining eyes, sitting at home and looking straight before her, like a piece of pure gold, too precious to touch.

Below them the river was glimmering, narrow, soft, and skin-colored, and slowed nearly to stillness. The shining willow trees hung round them. The net that was being drawn out, so old and so long-used, it too looked golden, strung and tied with golden threads.

Standing still on the bank, all of a sudden William Wallace, on whose word they were waiting, spoke up in a voice of surprise. "What is the name of this river?"

They looked at him as if he were crazy not to know the name of the river he had fished in all his life. But a deep frown was on his forehead, as if he were compelled to wonder what people had come to call this river, or to think there was a mystery in the name of a river they all knew so well, the same as if it were some great far torrent of waves that dashed through the mountains somewhere, and almost as if it were a river in some dream, for they could not give him the name of that.

"Everybody knows Pearl River is named the Pearl River," said Doc.

A bird note suddenly bold was like a stone thrown into the water to sound it.

"It's deep here," said Virgil, and jogged William Wallace. "Remember?"

William Wallace stood looking down at the river as if it were still a mystery to him. There under his feet which hung over the bank it was transparent and yellow like an old bottle lying in the sun, filling with light.

Doc clattered all his paraphernalia.

Then all of a sudden all the Malones scattered jumping and tumbling down the bank. They gave their loud shout. Little Brucie started after them, and looked back.

"Do you think she jumped?" Virgil asked William Wallace.

II

Since the net was so wide, when it was all stretched it reached from bank to bank of the Pearl River, and the weights would hold it all the way to the bottom. Jug-like sounds filled the air, splashes lifted in the sun, and the party began to move upstream. The Malones with great groans swam and pulled near the shore, the Doyles swam and pushed from behind with Virgil to tell them how to do it best; Grady and Brucie with his thread and pin trotted along the sandbars hauling buckets and lines. Sam and Robbie Bell, naked and bright, guided the old oarless rowboat that always drifted at the shore, and in it, sitting up tall with his hat on, was Doc—he went along without ever touching water and without ever taking his eyes off the net. William Wallace himself did everything but most of the time he was out of sight, swimming about under water or diving, and he had nothing to say any more.

The dogs chased up and down, in and out of the water, and in and out of the woods.

"Don't let her get too heavy, boys," Doc intoned regularly, every few minutes, "and she won't let nothing through."

"She won't let nothing through, she won't let nothing through," chanted Sam and Robbie Bell, one at his front and one at his back.

The sandbars were pink or violet drifts ahead. Where the light fell on the river, in a wandering from shore to shore, it was leaf-shaped spangles that trembled softly, while the dark of the river was calm. The willow trees leaned overhead under muscadine vines, and their trailing leaves hung like waterfalls in the morning air. The thing that seemed like silence must have been the endless cry of all the crickets and locusts in the world, rising and falling.

Every time William Wallace took hold of a big eel that slipped the net, the Malones all yelled, "Rassle with him, son!"

"Don't let her get too heavy, boys," said Doc.

"This is hard on catfish," William Wallace said once.

There were big and little fishes, dark and bright, that they caught, good ones and bad ones, the same old fish.

"This is more shoes than I ever saw got together in any store," said Virgil when they emptied the net to the bottom. "Get going!" he shouted in the next breath.

The little Rippens who had stayed ahead in the woods stayed ahead on the river. Brucie, leading them all, made small jumps and hops as he went, sometimes on one foot, sometimes on the other.

The winding river looked old sometimes, when it ran wrinkled and deep under high banks where the roots of trees hung down, and sometimes it seemed to be only a young creek, shining with the colors of wildflowers. Sometimes sandbars in the shapes of fishes lay nose to nose across, without the track of even a bird.

"Here comes some alligators," said Virgil. "Let's let them by."

They drew out on the shady side of the water, and three big alligators and four middle-sized ones went by, taking their own time.

"Look at their great big old teeth!" called a shrill voice. It was Grady making his only outcry,

and the alligators were not showing their teeth
at all.

"The better to eat folks with," said Doc from
his boat, looking at him severely.

"Doc, you are bound to declare all you know,"
said Virgil. "Get going!"

When they started off again the first thing they
caught in the net was the baby alligator.

"That's just what we wanted!" cried the Malones.

They set the little alligator down on a sandbar
and he squatted perfectly still; they could hardly
tell when it was he started to move. They watched
with set faces his incredible mechanics, while the
dogs after one bark stood off in inquisitive humility, until he winked.

"He's ours!" shouted all the Malones. "We're
taking him home with us!"

"He ain't nothing but a little-old baby," said
William Wallace.

The Malones only scoffed, as if he might be
only a baby but he looked like the oldest and
worst lizard.

"What are you going to do with him?" asked
Virgil.

"Keep him."

"I'd be more careful what I took out of this
net," said Doc.

"Tie him up and throw him in the bucket," the

Malones were saying to each other, while Doc was saying, "Don't come running to me and ask me what to do when he gets big."

They kept catching more and more fish, as if there was no end in sight.

"Look, a string of lady's beads," said Virgil. "Here, Sam and Robbie Bell."

Sam wore them around his head, with a knot over his forehead and loops around his ears, and Robbie Bell walked behind and stared at them.

In a shadowy place something white flew up. It was a heron, and it went away over the dark tree-tops. William Wallace followed it with his eyes and Brucie clapped his hands, but Virgil gave a sigh, as if he knew that when you go looking for what is lost, everything is a sign.

An eel slid out of the net.

"Rassle with him, son!" yelled the Malones. They swam like fiends.

"The Malones are in it for the fish," said Virgil.

It was about noon that there was a little rustle on the bank.

"Who is that yonder?" asked Virgil, and he pointed to a little undersized man with short legs and a little straw hat with a band around it, who was following along on the other side of the river.

"Never saw him and don't know his brother," said Doc.

Nobody had ever seen him before.

"Who invited you?" cried Virgil hotly. "Hi . . . !" and he made signs for the little undersized man to look at him, but he would not.

"Looks like a crazy man, from here," said the Malones.

"Just don't pay any attention to him and maybe he'll go away," advised Doc.

But Virgil had already swum across and was up on the other bank. He and the stranger could be seen exchanging a word apiece and then Virgil put out his hand the way he would pat a child and patted the stranger to the ground. The little man got up again just as quickly, lifted his shoulders, turned around, and walked away with his hat tilted over his eyes.

When Virgil came back he said, "Little-old man claimed he was harmless as a baby. I told him to just try horning in on this river and anything in it."

"What did he look like up close?" asked Doc.

"I wasn't studying how he looked," said Virgil. "But I don't like anybody to come looking at me that I am not familiar with." And he shouted, "Get going!"

"Things are moving in too great a rush," said Doc.

Brucie darted ahead and ran looking into all

the bushes, lifting up their branches and looking underneath.

"Not one of the Doyles has spoke a word," said Virgil.

"That's because they're not talkers," said Doc.

All day William Wallace kept diving to the bottom. Once he dived down and down into the dark water, where it was so still that nothing stirred, not even a fish, and so dark that it was no longer the muddy world of the upper river but the dark clear world of deepness, and he must have believed this was the deepest place in the whole Pearl River, and if she was not here she would not be anywhere. He was gone such a long time that the others stared hard at the surface of the water, through which the bubbles came from below. So far down and all alone, had he found Hazel? Had he suspected down there, like some secret, the real, the true trouble that Hazel had fallen into, about which words in a letter could not speak . . . how (who knew?) she had been filled to the brim with that elation that they all remembered, like their own secret, the elation that comes of great hopes and changes, sometimes simply of the harvest time, that comes with a little course of its own like a tune to run in the head, and there was nothing she could do about it —they knew—and so it had turned into this? It could be nothing but the old trouble that William Wallace was finding out, reaching and turning in the gloom of such depths.

"Look down yonder," said Grady softly to Brucie.

He pointed to the surface, where their reflections lay colorless and still side by side. He touched his brother gently as though to impress him.

"That's you and me," he said.

Brucie swayed precariously over the edge, and Grady caught him by the seat of his overalls. Brucie looked, but showed no recognition. Instead, he backed away, and seemed all at once unconcerned and spiritless, and pressed the nickel William Wallace had given him into his palm, rubbing it into his skin. Grady's inflamed eyes rested on the brown water. Without warning he saw something . . . perhaps the image in the river seemed to be his father, the drowned man—with arms open, eyes open, mouth open. . . . Grady stared and blinked, again something wrinkled up his face.

And when William Wallace came up it was in an agony from submersion, which seemed an agony of the blood and of the very heart, so woeful he looked. He was staring and glaring around in astonishment, as if a long time had gone by, away from the pale world where the brown light of the sun and the river and the little party watching him trembled before his eyes.

"What did you bring up?" somebody called—was it Virgil?

One of his hands was holding fast to a little green ribbon of plant, root and all. He was surprised, and let it go.

It was afternoon. The trees spread softly, the clouds hung wet and tinted. A buzzard turned a few slow wheels in the sky, and drifted upwards. The dogs promenaded the banks.

"It's time we ate fish," said Virgil.

On a wide sandbar on which seashells lay they dragged up the haul and built a fire.

Then for a long time among clouds of odors and smoke, all half-naked except Doc, they cooked and ate catfish. They ate until the Malones groaned and all the Doyles stretched out on their faces, though for long after, Sam and Robbie Bell sat up to their own little table on a cypress stump and ate on and on. Then they all were silent and still, and one by one fell asleep.

"There ain't a thing better than fish," muttered William Wallace. He lay stretched on his back in the glimmer and shade of trampled sand. His sunburned forehead and cheeks seemed to glow with fire. His eyelids fell. The shadow of a willow branch dipped and moved over him. "There is nothing in the world as good as . . . fish. The fish of Pearl River." Then slowly he smiled. He was asleep.

But it seemed almost at once that he was leaping up, and one by one up sat the others in their ring and looked at him, for it was impossible to stop and sleep by the river.

"You're feeling as good as you felt last night," said Virgil, setting his head on one side.

"The excursion is the same when you go looking for your sorrow as when you go looking for your joy," said Doc.

But William Wallace answered none of them anything, for he was leaping all over the place and all, over them and the feast and the bones of the feast, trampling the sand, up and down, and doing a dance so crazy that he would die next. He took a big catfish and hooked it to his belt buckle and went up and down so that they all hollered, and the tears of laughter streaming down his cheeks made him put his hand up, and the two days' growth of beard began to jump out, bright red.

But all of a sudden there was an even louder cry, something almost like a cheer, from everybody at once, and all pointed fingers moved from William Wallace to the river. In the center of three light-gold rings across the water was lifted first an old hoary head ("It has whiskers!" a voice cried) and then in an undulation loop after loop and hump after hump of a long dark body, until there were a dozen rings of ripples, one behind the other, stretching all across the river, like a necklace.

"The King of the Snakes!" cried all the Malones at once, in high tenor voices and leaning together.

"The King of the Snakes," intoned old Doc in his profound base.

"He looked you in the eye."

William Wallace stared back at the King of the Snakes with all his might.

It was Brucie that darted forward, dangling his little thread with the pin tied to it, going toward the water.

"That's the King of the Snakes!" cried Grady, who always looked after him.

Then the snake went down.

The little boy stopped with one leg in the air, spun around on the other, and sank to the ground.

"Git up," Grady whispered. "It was just the King of the Snakes. He went off whistling. Git up. It wasn't a thing but the King of the Snakes."

Brucie's green eyes opened, his tongue darted out, and he sprang up; his feet were heavy, his head light, and he rose like a bubble coming to the surface.

Then thunder like a stone loosened and rolled down the bank.

They all stood unwilling on the sandbar, holding to the net. In the eastern sky were the familiar castles and the round towers to which they were used, gray, pink, and blue, growing darker and filling with thunder. Lightning flickered in the sun along their thick walls. But in the west the sun shone with such a violence that in an illumination like a long-prolonged glare of lightning the heavens looked black and white; all color left the world, the goldenness of everything was like a memory, and only heat, a kind of glamor and oppression, lay on their heads. The thick heavy trees on the other side of the river were brushed with mile-long streaks of silver, and a wind touched each man on the forehead. At the same time there was a long roll of thunder that began behind them, came up and down mountains and valleys of air, passed over their heads, and left them listening still. With a small, near noise a mocking-bird followed it, the little white bars of its body flashing over the willow trees.

"We are here for a storm now," Virgil said. "We will have to stay till it's over."

They retreated a little, and hard drops fell in the leathery leaves at their shoulders and about their heads.

"Magnolia's the loudest tree there is in a storm," said Doc.

Then the light changed the water, until all about them the woods in the rising wind seemed to grow taller and blow inward together and suddenly turn dark. The rain struck heavily. A huge tail seemed to lash through the air and the river broke in a wound of silver. In silence the party crouched and stooped beside the trunk of the great tree, which in the push of the storm rose full of a fragrance and unyielding weight. Where they all stared, past their tree, was another tree, and beyond that another and another, all the way down the bank of the river, all towering and darkened in the storm.

"The outside world is full of endurance," said Doc. "Full of endurance."

Robbie Bell and Sam squatted down low and embraced each other from the start.

"Runs in our family to get struck by lightnin'," said Robbie Bell. "Lightnin' drawed a pitchfork right on our grandpappy's cheek, stayed till he died. Pappy got struck by some bolts of lightnin' and was dead three days, dead as that-there axe."

There was a succession of glares and crashes.

"This'n's goin' to be either me or you," said Sam. "Here come a little bug. If he go to the left, be me, and to the right, be you."

But at the next flare a big tree on the hill

seemed to turn into fire before their eyes, every branch, twig, and leaf, and a purple cloud hung over it.

"Did you hear that crack?" asked Robbie Bell. "That were its bones."

"Why do you little niggers talk so much!" said Doc. "Nobody's profiting by this information."

"We always talks this much," said Sam, "but now everybody so quiet, they hears us."

The great tree, split and on fire, fell roaring to earth. Just at its moment of falling, a tree like it on the opposite bank split wide open and fell in two parts.

"Hope they ain't goin' to be no balls of fire come rollin' over the water and fry all the fishes with they scales on," said Robbie Bell.

The water in the river had turned purple and was filled with sudden currents and whirlpools. The little willow trees bent almost to its surface, bowing one after another down the bank and almost breaking under the storm. A great curtain of wet leaves was borne along before a blast of wind, and every human being was covered.

"Now us got scales," wailed Sam. "Us is the fishes."

"Hush up, little-old colored children," said Virgil. "This isn't the way to act when somebody takes you out to drag a river."

"Poor lady's-ghost, I bet it is scareder than us," said Sam.

"All I hoping is, us don't find her!" screamed Robbie Bell.

William Wallace bent down and knocked their heads together. After that they clung silently in each other's arms, the two black heads resting, with wind-filled cheeks and tight-closed eyes, one upon the other until the storm was over.

"Right over yonder is Dover," said Virgil. "We've come all the way. William Wallace, you have walked on a sharp rock and cut your foot open."

III

In Dover it had rained, and the town looked somehow like new. The wavy heat of late afternoon came down from the watertank and fell over everything like shiny mosquito-netting. At the wide place where the road was paved and patched with tar, it seemed newly embedded with Coca-Cola tops. The old circus posters on the store were nearly gone, only bits, the snowflakes of white horses, clinging to its side. Morning-glory vines started almost visibly to grow over the roofs and cling round the ties of the railroad track, where bluejays lighted on the rails, and umbrella china-berry trees hung heavily over the whole town, dripping intermittently upon the tin roofs.

Each with his counted fish on a string the members of the river-dragging party walked through the town. They went toward the town well, and there was Hazel's mother's house, but no sign of her yet coming out. They all drank a dipper of the water, and still there was not a soul on the street. Even the bench in front of the store was empty, except for a little corn-shuck doll.

But something told them somebody had come, for after one moment people began to look out of the store and out of the postoffice. All the bird dogs woke up to see the Doyle dogs and such a large number of men and boys materialize suddenly with such a big catch of fish, and they ran out barking. The Doyle dogs joyously barked back. The bluejays flashed up and screeched above the town, whipping through their tunnels in the chinaberry trees. In the café a nickel clattered inside a music box and a love song began to play. The whole town of Dover began to throb in its wood and tin, like an old tired heart, when the men walked through once more, coming around again and going down the street carrying the fish, so drenched, exhausted, and muddy that no one could help but admire them.

William Wallace walked through the town as though he did not see anybody or hear anything. Yet he carried his great string of fish held high where it could be seen by all. Virgil came next, imitating William Wallace exactly, then the modest Doyles crowded by the Malones, who were holding up their alligator, tossing it in the air, even, like a father tossing his child. Following behind and pointing authoritatively at the ones in front strolled Doc, with Sam and Robbie Bell still chanting in his wake. In and out of the whole little line Grady and Brucie jerked about. Grady, with his head ducked, and stiff as a rod, walked with a springy limp; it made him look forever angry and unapproachable. Under his breath he was whispering, "Sty, sty, git out of my eye, and git on somebody passin' by." He traveled on with narrowed shoulders, and kept his eye unerringly upon his little brother, wary and at the same time proud, as though he held a flying Junebug on a string. Brucie, making a twanging noise with his lips, had shot forth again, and he was darting rapidly everywhere at once, delighted and tantalized, running in circles around William Wallace, pointing to his fish. A frown of pleasure like the print of a bird's foot was stamped between his faint brows, and he trotted in some unknown realm of delight.

"Did you ever see so many fish?" said the people in Dover.

"How much are your fish, mister?"

"Would you sell your fish?"

"Is that all the fish in Pearl River?"

"How much you sell them all for? Everybody's?"

"Three dollars," said William Wallace suddenly, and loud.

The Malones were upon him and shouting, but it was too late.

And just as William Wallace was taking the money in his hand, Hazel's mother walked solidly out of her front door and saw it.

"You can't head her mother off," said Virgil. "Here she comes in full bloom."

But William Wallace turned his back on her, that was all, and on everybody, for that matter, and that was the breaking-up of the party.

Just as the sun went down, Doc climbed his back steps, sat in his chair on the back porch where he sat in the evenings, and lighted his pipe. William Wallace hung out the net and came back and Virgil was waiting for him, so they could say good evening to Doc.

"All in all," said Doc, when they came up, "I've never been on a better river-dragging, or seen better behavior. If it took catching catfish to move the Rock of Gibraltar, I believe this outfit could move it."

"Well, we didn't catch Hazel," said Virgil.

"What did you say?" asked Doc.

"He don't really pay attention," said Virgil. "I said, 'We didn't catch Hazel.'"

"Who says Hazel was to be caught?" asked Doc. "She wasn't in there. Girls don't like the water—remember that. Girls don't just haul off and go jumping in the river to get back at their husbands. They got other ways."

"Didn't you ever think she was in there?" asked William Wallace. "The whole time?"

"Nary once," said Doc.

"He's just smart," said Virgil, putting his hand on William Wallace's arm. "It's only because we didn't find her that he wasn't looking for her."

"I'm beholden to you for the net, anyway," said William Wallace.

"You're welcome to borry it again," said Doc.

On the way home Virgil kept saying, "Calm down, calm down, William Wallace."

"If he wasn't such an old skinny man I'd have wrung his neck for him," said William Wallace. "He had no business coming."

"He's too big for his britches," said Virgil. "Don't nobody know everything. And just because it's his net. Why does it have to be his net?"

"If it wasn't for being polite to old men, I'd have skinned him alive," said William Wallace.

"I guess he don't really know nothing about wives at all, his wife's so deaf," said Virgil.

"He don't know Hazel," said William Wallace. "I'm the only man alive knows Hazel: would she jump in the river or not, and I say she would. She jumped in because I was sitting on the back of my neck in a ditch singing, and that's just what she ought to done. Doc ain't got no right to say one word about it."

"Calm down, calm down, William Wallace," said Virgil.

"If it had been you that talked like that, I'd have broke every bone in your body," said William Wallace. "Just let you talk like that. You're my age and size."

"But I ain't going to talk like that," said Virgil. "What have I done the whole time but keep this river-dragging going straight and running even, without no hitches? You couldn't have drug the river a foot without me."

"What are you talking about! Without who!" cried William Wallace. "This wasn't your river-dragging! It wasn't your wife!" He jumped on Virgil and they began to fight.

"Let me up." Virgil was breathing heavily.

"Say it was my wife. Say it was my river-dragging."

"Yours!" Virgil was on the ground with William Wallace's hand putting dirt in his mouth.

"Say it was my net."

"Your net!"

"Get up then."

They walked along getting their breath, and smelling the honeysuckle in the evening. On a hill William Wallace looked down, and at the same time there went drifting by the sweet sounds of music outdoors. They were having the Sacred Harp Sing on the grounds of an old white church glimmering there at the crossroads, far below. He stared away as if he saw it minutely, as if he could see a lady in white take a flowered cover off the organ, which was set on a little slant in the shade, dust the keys, and start to pump and play. . . . He smiled faintly, as he would at his mother, and at Hazel, and at the singing women in his life, now all one young girl standing up to sing under the trees the oldest and longest ballads there were.

Virgil told him good night and went into his own house and the door shut on him.

When he got to his own house, William Wallace saw to his surprise that it had not rained at all. But there, curved over the roof, was something he had never seen before as long as he could remember, a rainbow at night. In the light of the moon, which had risen again, it looked small and of gauzy material, like a lady's summer dress, a faint veil through which the stars showed.

He went up on the porch and in at the door, and all exhausted he had walked through the front room and through the kitchen when he heard his name called. After a moment, he smiled, as if no matter what he might have hoped for in his wildest heart, it was better than that to hear his name called out in the house. The voice came out of the bedroom.

"What do you want?" he yelled, standing stock-still.

Then she opened the bedroom door with the old complaining creak, and there she stood. She was not changed a bit.

"How do you feel?" he said.

"I feel pretty good. Not too good," Hazel said, looking mysterious.

"I cut my foot," said William Wallace, taking his shoe off so she could see the blood.

"How in the world did you do that?" she cried, with a step back.

"Dragging the river. But it don't hurt any longer."

"You ought to have been more careful," she said. "Supper's ready and I wondered if you would ever come home, or if it would be last night all over again. Go and make yourself fit to be seen," she said, and ran away from him.

After supper they sat on the front steps a while.

"Where were you this morning when I came in?" asked William Wallace when they were ready to go in the house.

"I was hiding," she said. "I was still writing on the letter. And then you tore it up."

"Did you watch me when I was reading it?"

"Yes, and you could have put out your hand and touched me, I was so close."

But he bit his lip, and gave her a little tap and slap, and then turned her up and spanked her.

"Do you think you will do it again?" he asked.

"I'll tell my mother on you for this!"

"Will you do it again?"

"No!" she cried.

"Then pick yourself up off my knee."

It was just as if he had chased her and captured her again. She lay smiling in the crook of his arm. It was the same as any other chase in the end.

"I will do it again if I get ready," she said. "Next time will be different, too."

Then she was ready to go in, and rose up and looked out from the top step, out across their yard where the China tree was and beyond, into the dark fields where the lightning-bugs flickered away. He climbed to his feet too and stood beside her, with the frown on his face, trying to look where she looked. And after a few minutes she took him by the hand and led him into the house, smiling as if she were smiling down on him.

A STILL MOMENT

 $\mathcal{L}$ ORENZO DOW rode the Old Natchez Trace at top speed upon a race horse, and the cry of the itinerant Man of God, "I must have souls! And souls I must have!" rang in his own windy ears. He rode as if never to stop, toward his night's appointment.

It was the hour of sunset. All the souls that he had saved and all those he had not took dusky shapes in the mist that hung between the high banks, and seemed by their great number and density to block his way, and showed no signs of melting or changing back into mist, so that he feared his passage was to be difficult forever. The poor souls that were not saved were darker and more pitiful than those that were, and still there was not any of the radiance he would have hoped to see in such a congregation.

"Light up, in God's name!" he called, in the pain of his disappointment.

Then a whole swarm of fireflies instantly flickered all around him, up and down, back and forth, first one golden light and then another, flashing without any of the weariness that had held back the souls. These were the signs sent from God that he had not seen the accumulated radiance of saved souls because he was not able, and that his eyes were more able to see the fire flies of the Lord than His blessed souls.

"Lord, give me the strength to see the angels when I am in Paradise," he said. "Do not let my eyes remain in this failing proportion to my loving heart always."

He gasped and held on. It was that day's complexity of horse-trading that had left him in the end with a Spanish race horse for which he was bound to send money in November from Georgia. Riding faster on the beast and still faster until he felt as if he were flying he sent thoughts of love with matching speed to his wife Peggy in Massachusetts. He found it effortless to love at a distance. He could look at the flowering trees and love Peggy in fullness, just as he could see his visions and love God. And Peggy, to whom he had not spoken until he could speak fateful words ("Would she accept of such an object as him?"), Peggy, the bride, with whom he had spent a few hours of time, showing of herself a small round handwriting, declared all in one letter, her first,

that she felt the same as he, and that the fear was
never of separation, but only of death.

Lorenzo well knew that it was Death that
opened underfoot, that rippled by at night, that
was the silence the birds did their singing in. He
was close to death, closer than any animal or bird.
On the back of one horse after another, winding
them all, he was always riding toward it or away
from it, and the Lord sent him directions with
protection in His mind.

Just then he rode into a thicket of Indians taking aim with their new guns. One stepped out and
took the horse by the bridle, it stopped at a touch,
and the rest made a closing circle. The guns
pointed.

"Incline!" The inner voice spoke sternly and
with its customary lightning-quickness.

Lorenzo inclined all the way forward and put
his head to the horse's silky mane, his body to its
body, until a bullet meant for him would endan-
ger the horse and make his death of no value.
Prone he rode out through the circle of Indians,
his obedience to the voice leaving him almost fear-
less, almost careless with joy.

But as he straightened and pressed ahead, care
caught up with him again. Turning half-beast and
half-divine, dividing himself like a heathen Cen-
taur, he had escaped his death once more. But
was it to be always by some metamorphosis of

himself that he escaped, some humiliation of his faith, some admission to strength and argumentation and not frailty? Each time when he acted so it was at the command of an instinct that he took at once as the word of an angel, until too late, when he knew it was the word of the devil. He had roared like a tiger at Indians, he had submerged himself in water blowing the savage bubbles of the alligator, and they skirted him by. He had prostrated himself to appear dead, and deceived bears. But all the time God would have protected him in His own way, less hurried, more divine.

Even now he saw a serpent crossing the Trace, giving out knowing glances.

He cried, "I know you now!", and the serpent gave him one look out of which all the fire had been taken, and went away in two darts into the tangle.

He rode on, all expectation, and the voices in the throats of the wild beasts went, almost without his noticing when, into words. "Praise God," they said. "Deliver us from one another." Birds especially sang of divine love which was the one ceaseless protection. "Peace, in peace," were their words so many times when they spoke from the briars, in a courteous sort of inflection, and he turned his countenance toward all perched creatures with a benevolence striving to match their own.

He rode on past the little intersecting trails, letting himself be guided by voices and by lights. It was battlesounds he heard most, sending him on, but sometimes ocean sounds, that long beat of waves that would make his heart pound and retreat as heavily as they, and he despaired again in his failure in Ireland when he took a voyage and persuaded with the Catholics with his back against the door, and then ran away to their cries of "Mind the white hat!" But when he heard singing it was not the militant and sharp sound of Wesley's hymns, but a soft, tireless and tender air that had no beginning and no end, and the softness of distance, and he had pleaded with the Lord to find out if all this meant that it was wicked, but no answer had come.

Soon night would descend, and a camp-meeting ground ahead would fill with its sinners like the sky with its stars. How he hungered for them! He looked in prescience with a longing of love over the throng that waited while the flames of the torches threw change, change, change over their faces. How could he bring them enough, if it were not divine love and sufficient warning of all that could threaten them? He rode on faster. He was a filler of appointments, and he filled more and more, until his journeys up and down creation were nothing but a shuttle, driving back and forth upon the rich expanse of his vision. He was homeless by his own choice, he must be everywhere at some time, and somewhere soon. There hastening in the wilderness on his flying horse he gave the night's torch-lit crowd a premature benediction, he could not wait. He spread his arms out, one at a time for safety, and he wished, when they would all be gathered in by his tin horn blasts and the inspired words would go out over their heads, to brood above the entire and passionate life of the wide world, to become its rightful part.

He peered ahead. "Inhabitants of Time! The wilderness is your souls on earth!" he shouted ahead into the treetops. "Look about you, if you would view the conditions of your spirit, put here by the good Lord to show you and afright you. These wild places and these trails of awesome loneliness lie nowhere, nowhere, but in your heart."

A dark man, who was James Murrell the outlaw, rode his horse out of a cane brake and began going along beside Lorenzo without looking at him. He had the alternately proud and aggrieved look of a man believing himself to be an instrument in the hands of a power, and when he was young he said at once to strangers that he was being used by Evil, or sometimes he stopped a traveler by shouting, "Stop! I'm the Devil!" He rode along now talking and drawing out his talk, by some deep control of the voice gradually slowing the speed of Lorenzo's horse down until both the horses were softly trotting. He would have wondered that nothing he said was heard, not knowing that Lorenzo listened only to voices of whose heavenly origin he was more certain.

Murrell riding along with his victim-to-be, Murrell riding, was Murrell talking. He told away at his long tales, with always a distance and a long length of time flowing through them, and all centered about a silent man. In each the silent man would have done a piece of evil, a robbery or a murder, in a place of long ago, and it was all made for the revelation in the end that the silent man was Murrell himself, and the long story had happened yesterday, and the place *here*—the Natchez Trace. It would only take one dawning look for the victim to see that all of this was another story and he himself had listened his way into it, and that he too was about to recede in time (to where the dread was forgotten) for some listener and to live for a listener in the long ago. Destroy the present!—that must have been the first thing that was whispered in Murrell's heart —the living moment and the man that lives in it must die before you can go on. It was his habit to

bring the journey—which might even take days—
to a close with a kind of ceremony. Turning his
face at last into the face of the victim, for he had
never seen him before now, he would tower up
with the sudden height of a man no longer the
tale teller but the speechless protagonist, silent at
last, one degree nearer the hero. Then he would
murder the man.

But it would always start over. This man going
forward was going backward with talk. He saw
nothing, observed no world at all. The two ends
of his journey pulled at him always and held him
in a nowhere, half asleep, smiling and witty,
dangling his predicament. He was a murderer
whose final stroke was over-long postponed, who
had to bring himself through the greatest tedium
to act, as if the whole wilderness, where he was
born, were his impediment. But behind him and
before him he kept in sight a victim, he saw a man
fixed and stayed at the point of death—no matter
how the man's eyes denied it, a victim, hands
spreading to reach as if for the first time for life.
Contempt! That is what Murrell gave that man.

Lorenzo might have understood, if he had not
been in haste, that Murrell in laying hold of a
man meant to solve his mystery of being. It was
as if other men, all but himself, would lighten
their hold on the secret, upon assault, and let it
fly free at death. In his violence he was only treat-

ing of enigma. The violence shook his own body
first, like a force gathering, and now he turned
in the saddle.

Lorenzo's despair had to be kindled as well as
his ecstasy, and could not come without that kin-
dling. Before the awe-filled moment when the
faces were turned up under the flares, as though
an angel hand tipped their chins, he had no way
of telling whether he would enter the sermon by
sorrow or by joy. But at this moment the face of
Murrell was turned toward him, turning at last,
all solitary, in its full, and Lorenzo would have
seized the man at once by his black coat and
shaken him like prey for a lost soul, so instantly
was he certain that the false fire was in his heart
instead of the true fire. But Murrell, quick when
he was quick, had put his own hand out, a re-
straining hand, and laid it on the wavelike flesh
of the Spanish race horse, which quivered and
shuddered at the touch.

They had come to a great live-oak tree at the
edge of a low marsh-land. The burning sun hung
low, like a head lowered on folded arms, and over
the long reaches of violet trees the evening
seemed still with thought. Lorenzo knew the place
from having seen it among many in dreams, and
he stopped readily and willingly. He drew rein, and
Murrell drew rein, he dismounted and Murrell
dismounted, he took a step, and Murrell was

there too; and Lorenzo was not surprised at the closeness, how Murrell in his long dark coat and over it his dark face darkening still, stood beside him like a brother seeking light.

But in that moment instead of two men coming to stop by the great forked tree, there were three.

From far away, a student, Audubon, had been approaching lightly on the wilderness floor, disturbing nothing in his lightness. The long day of beauty had led him this certain distance. A flock of purple finches that he tried for the first moment to count went over his head. He made a spelling of the soft *pet* of the ivory-billed woodpecker. He told himself always: remember.

Coming upon the Trace, he looked at the high cedars, azure and still as distant smoke overhead, with their silver roots trailing down on either side like the veins of deepness in this place, and he noted some fact to his memory—this earth that wears but will not crumble or slide or turn to dust, they say it exists in one other spot in the world, Egypt—and then forgot it. He walked quietly. All life used this Trace, and he liked to see the animals move along it in direct, oblivious journeys, for they had begun it and made it, the buffalo and deer and the small running creatures before man ever knew where he wanted to go, and birds flew a great mirrored course above.

Walking beneath them Audubon remembered how in the cities he had seen these very birds in his imagination, calling them up whenever he wished, even in the hard and glittering outer parlors where if an artist were humble enough to wait, some idle hand held up promised money. He walked lightly and he went as carefully as he had started at two that morning, crayon and paper, a gun, and a small bottle of spirits disposed about his body. (*Note: "The mocking birds so gentle that they would scarcely move out of the way."*) He looked with care; great abundance had ceased to startle him, and he could see things one by one. In Natchez they had told him of many strange and marvelous birds that were to be found here. Their descriptions had been exact, complete, and wildly varying, and he took them for inventions and believed that like all the worldly things that came out of Natchez, they would be disposed of and shamed by any man's excursion into the reality of Nature.

In the valley he appeared under the tree, a sure man, very sure and tender, as if the touch of all the earth rubbed upon him and the stains of the flowery swamp had made him so.

Lorenzo welcomed him and turned fond eyes upon him. To transmute a man into an angel was the hope that drove him all over the world and never let him flinch from a meeting or withhold good-byes for long. This hope insistently divided his life into only two parts, journey and rest. There could be no night and day and love and despair and longing and satisfaction to make partitions in the single ecstasy of this alternation. All things were speech.

"God created the world," said Lorenzo, "and it exists to give testimony. Life is the tongue: speak."

But instead of speech there happened a moment of deepest silence.

Audubon said nothing because he had gone without speaking a word for days. He did not regard his thoughts for the birds and animals as susceptible, in their first change, to words. His long playing on the flute was not in its origin a talking to himself. Rather than speak to order or describe, he would always draw a deer with a stroke across it to communicate his need of venison to an Indian. He had only found words when he discovered that there is much otherwise lost that can be noted down each item in its own day, and he wrote often now in a journal, not wanting anything to be lost the way it had been, all the past, and he would write about a day, "Only sorry that the Sun Sets."

Murrell, his cheated hand hiding the gun, could only continue to smile at Lorenzo, but he remembered in malice that he had disguised him-

self once as an Evangelist, and his final words to
this victim would have been, "One of my disguises
was what you are."

Then in Murrell Audubon he saw what he
thought of as "acquired sorrow"—that cumbrous-
ness and darkness from which the naked Indian,
coming just as he was made from God's hand, was
so lightly free. He noted the eyes—the dark kind
that loved to look through chinks, and saw neither
closeness nor distance, light nor shade, wonder
nor familiarity. They were narrowed to contract
the heart, narrowed to make an averting plan.
Audubon knew the finest-drawn tendons of the
body and the working of their power, for he had
touched them, and he supposed then that in man
the enlargement of the eye to see started a motion in the hands to make or do, and that the nar-
rowing of the eye stopped the hand and con-
tracted the heart. Now Murrell's eyes followed an
ant on a blade of grass, up the blade and down,
many times in the single moment. Audubon had
examined the Cave-In Rock where one robber
had lived his hiding life, and the air in the cave
was the cavelike air that enclosed this man, the
same odor, flinty and dark. O secret life, he
thought—is it true that the secret is withdrawn
from the true disclosure, that man is a cave man,
and that the openness I see, the ways through
forests, the rivers brimming light, the wide arches

where the birds fly, are dreams of freedom? If my origin is withheld from me, is my end to be unknown too? Is the radiance I see closed into an interval between two darks, or can it not illuminate them both and discover at last, though it cannot be spoken, what was thought hidden and lost?

In that quiet moment a solitary snowy heron flew down not far away and began to feed beside the marsh water.

At the single streak of flight, the ears of the race horse lifted, and the eyes of both horses filled with the soft lights of sunset, which in the next instant were reflected in the eyes of the men too as they all looked into the west toward the heron, and all eyes seemed infused with a sort of wildness.

Lorenzo gave the bird a triumphant look, such as a man may bestow upon his own vision, and thought, Nearness is near, lighted in a marsh-land, feeding at sunset. Praise God, His love has come visible.

Murrell, in suspicion pursuing all glances, blinking into a haze, saw only whiteness ensconced in darkness, as if it were a little luminous shell that drew in and held the eyesight. When he shaded his eyes, the brand "H.T." on his thumb thrust itself into his own vision, and he looked at the bird with the whole plan of the

Mystic Rebellion darting from him as if in rays of the bright reflected light, and he stood looking proudly, leader as he was bound to become of the slaves, the brigands and outcasts of the entire Natchez country, with plans, dates, maps burning like a brand into his brain, and he saw himself proudly in a moment of prophecy going down rank after rank of successively bowing slaves to unroll and flaunt an awesome great picture of the Devil colored on a banner.

Audubon's eyes embraced the object in the distance and he could see it as carefully as if he held it in his hand. It was a snowy heron alone out of its flock. He watched it steadily, in his care noting the exact inevitable things. When it feeds it muddies the water with its foot. . . . It was as if each detail about the heron happened slowly in time, and only once. He felt again the old stab of wonder—what structure of life bridged the reptile's scale and the heron's feather? That knowledge too had been lost. He watched without moving. The bird was defenseless in the world except for the intensity of its life, and he wondered, how can heat of blood and speed of heart defend it? Then he thought, as always as if it were new and unbelievable, it has nothing in space or time to prevent its flight. And he waited, knowing that some birds will wait for a sense of their presence to travel to men before they will fly away from them.

Fixed in its pure white profile it stood in the precipitous moment, a plumicorn on its head, its breeding dress extended in rays, eating steadily the little water creatures. There was a little space between each man and the others, where they stood overwhelmed. No one could say the three had ever met, or that this moment of intersection had ever come in their lives, or its promise fulfilled. But before them the white heron rested in the grasses with the evening all around it, lighter and more serene than the evening, flight closed in its body, the circuit of its beauty closed, a bird seen and a bird still, its motion calm as if it were offered: Take my flight. . . .

What each of them had wanted was simply *all*. To save all souls, to destroy all men, to see and to record all life that filled this world—all, all— but now a single frail yearning seemed to go out of the three of them for a moment and to stretch toward this one snowy, shy bird in the marshes. It was as if three whirlwinds had drawn together at some center, to find there feeding in peace a snowy heron. Its own slow spiral of flight could take it away in its own time, but for a little it held them still, it laid quiet over them, and they stood for a moment unburdened. . . .

Murrell wore no mask, for his face was that, a face that was aware while he was somnolent, a face that watched for him, and listened for him, alert and nearly brutal, the guard of a planner. He was quick without that he might be slow within, he staved off time, he wandered and plotted, and yet his whole desire mounted in him toward the end (was this the end—the sight of a bird feeding at dusk?), toward the instant of confession. His incessant deeds were thick in his heart now, and flinging himself to the ground he thought wearily, when all these trees are cut down, and the Trace lost, then my Conspiracy that is yet to spread itself will be disclosed, and all the stone-loaded bodies of murdered men will be pulled up, and all everywhere will know poor Murrell. His look pressed upon Lorenzo, who stared upward, and Audubon, who was taking out his gun, and his eyes squinted up to them in pleading, as if to say, "How soon may I speak, and how soon will you pity me?" Then he looked back to the bird, and he thought if it would look at him a dread penetration would fill and gratify his heart.

Audubon in each act of life was aware of the mysterious origin he half-concealed and half-sought for. People along the way asked him in their kindness or their rudeness if it were true, that he was born a prince, and was the Lost Dauphin, and some said it was his secret, and some said that that was what he wished to find out before he died. But if it was his identity that he wished to discover, or if it was what a man

had to seize beyond that, the way for him was by
endless examination, by the care for every bird
that flew in his path and every serpent that shone
underfoot. Not one was enough; he looked deeper
and deeper, on and on, as if for a particular beast
or some legendary bird. Some men's eyes persisted
in looking outward when they opened to look inward, and to their delight, there outflung was the
astonishing world under the sky. When a man at
last brought himself to face some mirror-surface
he still saw the world looking back at him, and if
he continued to look, to look closer and closer,
what then? The gaze that looks outward must be
trained without rest, to be indomitable. It must
see as slowly as Murrell's ant in the grass, as ex-
haustively as Lorenzo's angel of God, and then,
Audubon dreamed, with his mind going to his
pointed brush, it must see like this, and he tight-
ened his hand on the trigger of the gun and
pulled it, and his eyes went closed. In memory
the heron was all its solitude, its total beauty. All
its whiteness could be seen from all sides at once,
its pure feathers were as if counted and known
and their array one upon the other would never
be lost. But it was not from that memory that he
could paint.

His opening eyes met Lorenzo's, close and flashing, and it was on seeing horror deep in them, like
fires in abysses, that he recognized it for the first

time. He had never seen horror in its purity and clarity until now, in bright blue eyes. He went and picked up the bird. He had thought it to be a female, just as one sees the moon as female; and so it was. He put it in his bag, and started away. But Lorenzo had already gone on, leaning a-tilt on the horse which went slowly.

Murrell was left behind, but he was proud of the dispersal, as if he had done it, as if he had always known that three men in simply being together and doing a thing can, by their obstinacy, take the pride out of one another. Each must go away alone, each send the others away alone. He himself had purposely kept to the wildest country in the world, and would have sought it out, the loneliest road. He looked about with satisfaction, and hid. Travelers were forever innocent, he believed: that was his faith. He lay in wait; his faith was in innocence and his knowledge was of ruin; and had these things been shaken? Now, what could possibly be outside his grasp? Churning all about him like a cloud about the sun was the great folding descent of his thought. Plans of deeds made his thoughts, and they rolled and mingled about his ears as if he heard a dark voice that rose up to overcome the wilderness voice, or was one with it. The night would soon come; and he had gone through the day.

Audubon, splattered and wet, turned back into

the wilderness with the heron warm under his hand, his head still light in a kind of trance. It was undeniable, on some Sunday mornings, when he turned over and over his drawings they seemed beautiful to him, through what was dramatic in the conflict of life, or what was exact. What he would draw, and what he had seen, became for a moment one to him then. Yet soon enough, and it seemed to come in that same moment, like Lorenzo's horror and the gun's firing, he knew that even the sight of the heron which surely he alone had appreciated, had not been all his belonging, and that never could any vision, even any simple sight, belong to him or to any man. He knew that the best he could make would be, after it was apart from his hand, a dead thing and not a live thing, never the essence, only a sum of parts; and that it would always meet with a stranger's sight, and never be one with the beauty in any other man's head in the world. As he had seen the bird most purely at its moment of death, in some fatal way, in his care for looking outward, he saw his long labor most revealingly at the point where it met its limit. Still carefully, for he was trained to see well in the dark, he walked on into the deeper woods, noting all sights, all sounds, and was gentler than they as he went.

In the woods that echoed yet in his ears, Lorenzo riding slowly looked back. The hair rose on his head and his hands began to shake with cold, and suddenly it seemed to him that God Himself, just now, thought of the Idea of Separateness. For surely He had never thought of it before, when the little white heron was flying down to feed. He could understand God's giving Separateness first and then giving Love to follow and heal in its wonder; but God had reversed this, and given Love first and then Separateness, as though it did not matter to Him which came first. Perhaps it was that God never counted the moments of Time; Lorenzo did that, among his tasks of love. Time did not occur to God. Therefore—did He even know of it? How to explain Time and Separateness back to God, Who had never thought of them, Who could let the whole world come to grief in a scattering moment?

Lorenzo brought his cold hands together in a clasp and stared through the distance at the place where the bird had been as if he saw it still; as if nothing could really take away what had happened to him, the beautiful little vision of the feeding bird. Its beauty had been greater than he could account for. The sweat of rapture poured down from his forehead, and then he shouted into the marshes.

"Tempter!"

He whirled forward in the saddle and began to hurry the horse to its high speed. His camp ground was far away still, though even now they must be lighting the torches and gathering in the multitudes, so that at the appointed time he would duly appear in their midst, to deliver his address on the subject of "In that day when all hearts shall be disclosed."

Then the sun dropped below the trees, and the new moon, slender and white, hung shyly in the west.

ASPHODEL

$\mathcal{I}$T WAS a cloudless day—a round
hill where the warm winds blew. It was noon,
and without a shadow the line of columns rose
in perfect erectness from the green vines. There
was a quiver of birdsong. A little company of
three women stood fixed on the slope before
the ruin, holding wicker baskets between them.
They were not young. There were identical looks
of fresh mourning on their faces. A wind blew
down from the columns, and the white dimity
fluttered about their elbows.

"Look—"

"Asphodel."

It was a golden ruin: six Doric columns, with
the entablature unbroken over the first two, full-
facing the approach. The sky was pure, transparent, and round like a shell over this hill.

The three women drew nearer, in postures that
were still from ministrations, and that came from
a mourning procession.

"This is Asphodel," they repeated, looking modestly upward to the frieze of maidens that was saturated with sunlight and seemed to fill with color, and before which the branch of a leafy tree was trembling.

"If there's one place in the solid world where Miss Sabina would never look for us, it's Asphodel," they said. "She forbade it," they said virtuously. "She would never tolerate us to come, to Mr. Don McInnis's Asphodel, or even to say his name."

"Her funeral was yesterday, and we've cried our eyes dry," said one of the three. "And as for saying Mr. Don's name out loud, of course he is dead too." And they looked from one to the other —Cora, Phoebe, and Irene, all old maids, in hanging summer cottons, carrying picnic baskets. The way was so narrow they had come in a buggy, then walked.

There was not a shadow. It was high noon. A honey locust bent over their heads, sounding with the bees that kept at its bee-like flowers.

"This is the kind of day I could just *eat!*" cried Cora ardently.

They were another step forward. A little stream spread from rock to rock and over the approach. Then their shoes were off, and their narrow maiden feet hung trembling in the rippling water.

The wind had shaken loose their gray and scanty hair. They smiled at one another.

"I used to be scared of little glades," said Phoebe. "I used to think something, something wild, would come and carry me off."

Then they were laughing freely all at once, drying their feet on the other side of the stream. The mocking-birds seemed to imitate flutes in the midday air. The horse they had unhitched champed on the hill, always visible—an old horse that seemed about to run, his mane fluttering in the light and his tail flaunted like a decoration he had only just put on.

Then the baskets were opened, the cloth was spread with the aromatic ham and chicken, spices and jellies, fresh breads and a cake, peaches, bananas, figs, pomegranates, grapes, and a thin dark bottle of blackberry cordial.

"There's one basket left in the buggy," said Irene, always the last to yield. "I like to have a little something saved back."

The women reclined before the food, beside the warm and weighty pedestal. Above them the six columns seemed to be filled with the inhalations of summer and to be suspended in the resting of noon.

They pressed at the pomegranate stains on their mouths. And then they began to tell over

Miss Sabina's story, their voices serene and alike: how she looked, the legend of her beauty when she was young, the house where she was born and what happened in it, and how she came out when she was old, and her triumphal way, and the pitiful end when she toppled to her death in a dusty place where she was a stranger, that she had despised and deplored.

"Miss Sabina's house stood on the high hill," Cora said, but the lips of the others moved with hers. It was like an old song they carried in their memory, the story of the two houses separated by a long, winding, difficult, untravelled road—a curve of the old Natchez Trace—but actually situated almost back to back on the ring of hills, while completely hidden from each other, like the reliefs on opposite sides of a vase.

"It commanded the town that came to be at its foot. Her house was a square of marble and stone, the front was as dark as pitch under the magnolia trees. Not one blade of grass grew in the hard green ground, but in some places a root stuck up like a serpent. Inside, the house was all wood, dark wood carved and fluted, long hallways, great staircases of walnut, ebony beds that filled a room, even mahogany roses in the ceilings, where the chandeliers hung down like red glass fruit. There was one completely dark inside room. The house was a labyrinth set with statues—Venus, Hermes,

Demeter, and with singing ocean shells on draped pedestals.

"Miss Sabina's father came bringing Mr. Don McInnis home, and proposed the marriage to him. She was no longer young for suitors; she was instructed to submit. On the marriage night the house was ablaze, and lighted the town and the wedding guests climbing the hill. We were there. The presents were vases of gold, gold cups, statues of Diana. . . . And the bride . . . We had not forgotten it yesterday when we drew it from the chest—the stiff white gown she wore! It never made a rustle when she gave him her hand. It was spring, the flowers in the baskets were purple hyacinths and white lilies that wilted in the heat and showed their blue veins. Ladies fainted from the scent; the gentlemen were without exception drunk, and Mr. Don McInnis, with his head turning quickly from side to side, like an animal's, opened his mouth and laughed."

Irene said: "A great, profane man like all the McInnis men of Asphodel, Mr. Don McInnis. He was the last of his own, just as she was the last of hers. The hope was in him, and he knew it. He had a sudden way of laughter, like a rage, that pointed his eyebrows that were yellow, and changed his face. That night he stood astride . . . astride the rooms, the guests, the flowers, the ta·

pers, the bride and her father with his purple face. 'What, Miss Sabina?' he would roar, though she had never said a word, not one word . . . waiting in the stiffened gown that took then its odor of burning wax. We remembered that, that roar, that 'What, Miss Sabina?' and we whispered it among ourselves later when we embroidered together, as though it were a riddle that young ladies could not answer. He seemed never to have said any other thing to her. He was dangerous that first night, swaying with drink, trampling the scattered flowers, led up to a ceremony there before all our eyes, Miss Sabina so rigid by his side. He was a McInnis, a man that would be like a torch carried into a house."

The three old maids, who lay like a faded garland at the foot of the columns, paused in peaceful silence. When the story was taken up again, it was in Phoebe's delicate and gentle way, for its narrative was only part of memory now, and its beginning and ending might seem mingled and freed in the blue air of the hill.

"She bore three children, two boys and a girl, and one by one they died as they reached maturity. There was Minerva and she was drowned— before her wedding day. There was Theo, coming out from the university in his gown of the law, and killed in a fall off the wild horse he was bound to ride. And there was Lucian the youngest, shooting himself publicly on the courthouse steps, drunk in the broad daylight.

"Who can tell what will happen in this world!" said Phoebe, and she looked placidly up into the featureless sky overhead.

"It all served to make Miss Sabina prouder than ever," Irene said. "She was born grand, with a will to impose, and now she had only Mr. Don left, to impose it upon. But he was a McInnis. He had the wildness we all worshipped that first night, since he was not to be ours to love. He was unfaithful—maybe always—maybe once—"

"We told the news," said Cora. "We went in a body up the hill and into the house, weeping and wailing, hardly daring to name the name or the deed."

"It was in the big hall by the statues of the Seasons, and she stood up to listen to us all the way through," Irene murmured. "She didn't move— she didn't blink her eye. We stood there in our little half-circle not daring to come closer. Then she reached out both her arms as though she would embrace us all, and made fists with her hands, with the sharp rings cutting into her, and called down the curse of heaven on everybody's head—his, and the woman's, and the dead children's, and ours. Then she walked out, and the door of her bedroom closed."

"We ran away," said Phoebe languidly. "We ran down the steps and in and out of the boxwood garden, around the fountain, all clutching one another as though we were pursued, and away through the street, crying. She never shed a tear, whatever happened, but we shed enough for everybody."

Cora said: "By that time, her father was dead and there was no one to right the wrong. And Mr. Don—he only flourished. He wore white linen suits summer and winter. She declared the lightning would strike him for the destruction he had brought on her, but it never struck. She never closed her eyes a single night, she was so outraged and so undone. She would not eat a bite for anybody. We carried things up to her—soups, birds, wines, frozen surprises, cold shapes, one after the other. She only pushed them away. It could have been thought that life with the beast was the one thing in the living world to be pined after. But 'How can I hate him enough?' she said over and over. 'How can I show him the hate I have for him?' She implored us to tell her."

"We heard he was running away to Asphodel," said Irene, "and taking the woman. And when we went and told Miss Sabina, she would not wait any longer for an act of God to punish him, though we took her and held her till she pushed us from her side."

"She drove Mr. Don out of the house," said Cora, to whom the cordial was now passed. "Drove him out with a whip, in the broad daylight. It was a day like this, in summer—I remember the magnolias that made the air so heavy and full of sleep. It was just after dinner time and all the population came out and stood helpless to see, as if in a dream. Like a demon she sprang from the door and rushed down the long iron steps, driving him before her with the buggy whip, that had a purple tassel. He walked straight ahead as if to humor her, with his white hat lifted and held in his hand."

"We followed at a little distance behind her, in case she should faint," said Phoebe. "But we were the ones who were near to fainting, when she set her feet in the gateway after driving him through, and called at the top of her voice for the woman to come forward. She longed to whip her there and then. But no one came forward. She swore that we were hiding and protecting some wretched creature, that we were all in league. Miss Sabina put a great blame on the whole town."

"When Asphodel burned that night," said Cora, "and we all saw the fire raging on the sky, we ran and told her, and she was gratified—but from that moment remote from us and grand. And she laid down the law that the name of Don

McInnis and the name of Asphodel were not to cross our lips again. . . ."

The prodigious columns shone down and appeared tremulous with the tender light of summer which enclosed them all around, in equal and shadowless flame. They seemed to flicker with the flight of birds.

"Miss Sabina," said Irene, "for the rest of her life was proceeding through the gateway and down the street, and all her will was turned upon the population."

"She was painted to be beautiful and terrible in the face, all dark around the eyes," said Phoebe, "in the way of grand ladies of the South grown old. She wore a fine jet-black wig of great size, for she had lost her hair by some illness or violence. She went draped in the heavy brocades from her family trunks, which she hung about herself in some bitter disregard. She would do no more than pin them and tie them into place. Through such a weight of material her knees pushed slowly, her progress was hampered but she came on. Her look was the challenging one when looks met, though only Miss Sabina knew why there had to be any clangor of encounter among peaceable people. *We* knew she had been beautiful. Her hands were small, and as hot to the touch as a child's under the sharp diamonds. One hand, the right one, curved round and clenched an ebony stick mounted with the gold head of a lion."

"She took her stick and went down the street proclaiming and wielding her power," said Cora. "Her power reached over the whole population—white and black, men and women, children, idiots, and animals—even strangers. Her law was laid over us, her riches were distributed upon us; we were given a museum and a statue, a waterworks. And we stood in fear of her, old and young and like ourselves. At the May Festival when she passed by, all the maypoles became hopelessly tangled, one by one. Her good wish and her censure could be as clearly told apart as a white horse from a black one. All news was borne to her first, and she interrupted every news-bearer. 'You don't have to tell me: I know. The woman is dead. The child is born. The man is proved a thief.' There would be a time when she appeared at the door of every house on the street, pounding with her cane. She dominated every ceremony, set the times for weddings and for funerals, even for births, and she named the children. She ordered lives about and moved people from one place to another in the town, brought them together or drove them apart, with the mystical and rigorous devotion of a priestess in a story; and she prophesied all the things beforehand. She foretold disaster, and was ready with hot breads and soups to send by running Negroes to every house the moment it struck. And she expected her imparted recipes to be used forever after, and no other. We are eating Miss Sabina's cake now. . . ."

"But at the end of the street there was one door where Miss Sabina had never entered," said Phoebe. "The door of the post office. She acted as if the post office had no existence in the world, or else she called it a dirty little room with the door standing wide open to the flies. All the hate she had left in her when she was old went out to a little four-posted whitewashed building, the post office. It was beyond her domain. For there we might still be apart in a dream, and she did not know what it was."

"But in the end, she came in," said Irene.

"We were there," she said. "It was mail time, and we each had a letter in our hands. We heard her come to the end of the street, the heavy staggering figure coming to the beat of the cane. We were silent all at once. When Miss Sabina is at the door, there is no other place in the world but where you stand, and no other afternoon but that one, past or future. We held onto our letters as onto all far-away or ephemeral things at that moment, to our secret hope or joy and our despair too, which she might require of us."

"When she entered," said Cora, "and took her

stand in the center of the floor, a little dog saw who it was and trotted out, and alarm like the vibration from the firebell trembled in the motes of the air, and the crowded room seemed to shake, to totter. We looked at one another in greater fear of her than ever before in our lives, and we would have run away or spoken to her first, except for a premonition that this time was the last, this demand the final one."

"It was as if the place of the smallest and the longest-permitted indulgence, the little common green, were to be invaded when the time came for the tyrant to die," said Phoebe.

The three old maids sighed gently. The grapes they held upon their palms were transparent in the light, so that the little black seeds showed within.

"But when Miss Sabina spoke," said Irene, "she said, 'Give me my letter.' And Miss Sabina never got a letter in her life. She never knew a soul beyond the town. We told her there was no letter for her, but she cried out again, 'Give me my letter!' We told her there was none, and we went closer and tried to gather her to us. But she said, 'Give me that.' And she took our letters out of our hands. 'Your lovers!' she said, and tore them in two. We let her do just as she would. But she was not satisfied. 'Open up!' she said to the post-mistress, and she beat upon the little communicating door. So the postmistress had to open up, and Miss Sabina went in to the inner part. We all drew close. We glanced at one another with our eyes grown bright, like people under a spell, for she was bent upon destruction."

"A fury and a pleasure seemed to rise inside her, that went out like lightning through her hands," said Cora. "She threw down her stick, she advanced with her bare hands. She seized upon everything before her, and tore it to pieces. She dragged the sacks about, and the wastebaskets, and the contents she scattered like snow. Even the ink pad she flung against the wall, and it left a purple mark like a grape stain that will never wear off.

"She was possessed then, before our eyes, as she could never have been possessed. She raged. She rocked from side to side, she danced. Miss Sabina's arms moved like a harvester's in the field, to destroy all that was in the little room. In her frenzy she tore all the letters to pieces, and even put bits in her mouth and appeared to eat them.

"Then she stood still in the little room. She had finished. We had not yet moved when she lay toppled on the floor, her wig fallen from her head and her face awry like a mask.

" 'A stroke.' That is what we said, because we did not know how to put a name to the end of her life. . . ."

Here in the bright sun where the three old maids sat beside their little feast, Miss Sabina's was an old story, closed and complete. In some intoxication of the time and the place, they recited it and came to the end. Now they lay stretched on their sides on the ground, their summer dresses spread out, little smiles forming on their mouths, their eyes half-closed, Phoebe with a juicy green leaf between her teeth. Above them like a dream rested the bright columns of Asphodel, a dream like the other side of their lamentations.

All at once there was a shudder in the vines growing up among the columns. Out into the radiant light with one foot forward had stepped a bearded man. He stood motionless as one of the columns, his eyes bearing without a break upon the three women. He was as rude and golden as a lion. He did nothing, and he said nothing while the birds sang on. But he was naked.

The white picnic cloth seemed to have stirred of itself and spilled out the half-eaten fruit and shattered the bottle of wine as the three old maids first knelt, then stood, and with a cry clung with their arms upon one another. As if they heard a sound in the vibrant silence, they were compelled to tarry in the very act of flight. In a soft little chorus of screams they waited, looking back over their shoulders, with their arms stretched before them. Then their shoes were left behind them, and the three made a little line across the brook, and across the field in an aisle that opened among the mounds of wild roses. With the suddenness of birds they had all dropped to earth at the same moment and as if by magic risen on the other side of the fence, beside a "No Trespassing" sign.

They stood wordless together, brushing and plucking at their clothes, while quite leisurely the old horse trotted towards them across this pasture that was still, for him, unexplored.

The bearded man had not moved once.

Cora spoke. "That was Mr. Don McInnis."

"It was not," said Irene. "It was a vine in the wind."

Phoebe was bent over to pull a thorn from her bare foot. "But we thought he was dead."

"That was just as much Mr. Don as this is I," said Cora, "and I would swear to that in a court of law."

"He was naked," said Irene.

"He was buck-naked," said Cora. "He was as naked as an old goat. He must be as old as the hills."

"I didn't look," declared Phoebe. But there at one side she stood bowed and trembling as if from a fateful encounter.

"No need to cry about it, Phoebe," said Cora. "If it's Mr. Don, it's Mr. Don."

They consoled one another, and hitched the

horse, and then waited still in their little cluster, looking back.

"What Miss Sabina wouldn't have given to see him!" cried Cora at last. "What she wouldn't have told him, what she wouldn't have done to him!"

But at that moment, as their gaze was fixed on the ruin, a number of goats appeared between the columns of Asphodel, and with a little leap started down the hill. Their nervous little hooves filled the air with a shudder and palpitation.

"Into the buggy!"

Tails up, the goats leapt the fence as if there was nothing they would rather do.

Cora, Irene, and Phoebe were inside the open buggy, the whip was raised over the old horse.

"There are more and more coming still," cried Irene.

There were billy-goats and nanny-goats, old goats and young, a whole thriving herd. Their little beards all blew playfully to the side in the wind of their advancement.

"They are bound to catch up," cried Irene.

"Throw them something," said Cora, who held the reins.

At their feet was the basket that had been saved out, with a napkin of biscuits and bacon on top.

"Here, billy-goats!" they cried.

Leaning from the sides of the buggy, their

sleeves fluttering, each one of them threw back biscuits with both hands.

"Here, billy-goats!" they cried, but the little goats were prancing so close, their inquisitive noses were almost in the spokes of the wheels.

"It won't stop them," said Phoebe. "They're not satisfied in the least, it only makes them curious."

Cora was standing up in the open buggy, driving it like a chariot. "Give them the little baked hen, then," she said, and they threw it behind.

The little goats stopped, with their heads flecked to one side, and then their horns met over the prize.

There was a turn, and Asphodel was out of sight. The road went into a ravine and wound into the shade. . . .

"We escaped," said Cora.

"I am thankful Miss Sabina did not live to see us then," said Irene. "She would have been ashamed of us—barefooted and running. She would never have given up the little basket we had saved back."

"He ought not to be left at liberty," cried Cora. She spoke soothingly to the old horse whose haunches still trembled, and then said, "I have a good mind to report him to the law!"

There was the great house where Miss Sabina had lived, high on the coming hill.

But Phoebe laughed aloud as they made the curve. Her voice was soft, and she seemed to be still in a tender dream and an unconscious cele- bration—as though the picnic were not already set rudely in the past, but were the enduring and in- toxicating present, still the phenomenon, the golden day.

THE WINDS

HEN Josie first woke up in the night she thought the big girls of the town were having a hay-ride. Choruses and cries of what she did not question to be joy came stealing through the air. At once she could see in her mind the source of it, the Old Natchez Trace, which was at the edge of her town, an old dark place where the young people went, and it was called both things, the Old Natchez Trace and Lover's Lane. An excitement touched her and she could see in her imagination the leaning wagon coming, the long white-stockinged legs of the big girls hung down in a fringe on one side of the hay—then as the horses made a turn, the boys' black stockings stuck out the other side.

But while her heart rose longingly to the pitch of their delight, hands reached under her and she was lifted out of bed.

"Don't be frightened," said her father's voice into her ear, as if he told her a secret.

Am I old? Am I invited? she wondered, stricken.

The chorus seemed to envelop her, but it was her father's thin nightshirt she lay against in the dark.

"I still say it's a shame to wake them up." It was her mother's voice coming from the doorway, though strangely argumentative for so late in the night.

Then they were all moving in the stirring darkness, all in their nightgowns, she and Will being led by their mother and father, and they in turn with their hands out as if they were being led by something invisible. They moved off the sleeping porch into the rooms of the house. The calls and laughter of the older children came closer, and Josie thought that at any moment their voices would all come together, and they would sing their favorite round, "Row, row, row your boat, gently down the stream—merrily, merrily, merrily, merrily—"

"Don't turn on the lights," said her father, as if to keep the halls and turnings secret within. They passed the front bedroom; she knew it by the scent of her mother's verbena sachet and the waist-shape of the mirror which showed in the dark. But they did not go in there. Her father put little coats about them, not their right ones. In her sleep she seemed to have dreamed the sounds

of all the windows closing, upstairs and down.
Coming out of the guest-room was a sound like a
nest of little mice in the hay; in a flash of pride
and elation Josie discovered it to be the empty
bed rolling around and squeaking on its wheels.
Then close beside them was a small musical
tinkle against the floor, and she knew the sound;
it was Will's Tinker-Toy tower coming apart and
the wooden spools and rods scattering down.

"Oh boy!" cried Will, spreading his arms high
in his sleep and beginning to whirl about. "The
house is falling down!"

"Hush," said their mother, catching him.

"Never mind," said their father, smoothing
Josie's hair but speaking over her head. "Down-
stairs."

The hour had never seemed so late in their
house as when they made this slow and unsteady
descent. Josie thought again of Lover's Lane. The
stairway gave like a chain, the pendulum shivered
in the clock.

They moved into the living room. The summer
matting was down on the floor, cracked and lying
in little ridges under their sandals, smelling of its
stains and dust, of thin green varnish, and of its
origin in China. The sheet of music open on the
piano had caved in while they slept, and gleamed
faintly like a shell in the shimmer and flow of the
strange light. Josie's drawing of the plaster-cast of

Joan of Arc, which it had taken her all summer to do for her mother, had rolled itself tightly up on the desk like a diploma. Were they all going away and leave that? They wandered separately for a moment looking like strangers at the wicker chairs. The cretonne pillows smelled like wet stones. Outside the beseeching cries rose and fell, and drew nearer. The curtains hung almost still, like poured cream, down the windows, but on the table the petals shattered all at once from a bowl of roses. Then the chorus of wildness and delight seemed to come almost into their street, though still it held its distance, exactly like the wandering wagon filled with the big girls and boys at night.

Will in his little shirt was standing straight up with his eyes closed, erect as a spinning top.

"He'll sleep through it," said their mother. "You take him, and I'll take the girl." With a little push, she divided the children; she was unlike herself. Then their mother and father sat down opposite each other in the wicker chairs. They were waiting.

"Is it a moonlight picnic?" asked Josie.

"It's a storm," said her father. He answered her questions formally in a kind of deep courtesy always, which did not depend on the day or night. "This is the equinox."

Josie gave a leap at that and ran to the front window and looked out.

"Josie!"

She was looking for the big girl who lived in the double-house across the street. There was a strange fluid lightning which she now noticed for the first time to be filling the air, violet and rose, and soundless of thunder; and the eyes of the double-house seemed to open and shut with it.

"Josie, come back."

"I see Cornella. I see Cornella in the equinox, there in her high-heeled shoes."

"Nonsense," said her father. "Nonsense, Josie."

But she stood with her back to all of them and looked, saying, "I see Cornella."

"How many times have I told you that you need not concern yourself with—Cornella!" The way her mother said her name was not diminished now.

"I see Cornella. She's on the outside, Mama, outside in the storm, and she's in the equinox."

But her mother would not answer.

"Josie, don't you understand—I want to keep us close together," said her father. She looked back at him. "Once in an equinoctial storm," he said cautiously over the sleeping Will, "a man's little girl was blown away from him into a haystack out in a field."

"The wind will come after Cornella," said Josie.

But he called her back.

The house shook as if a big drum were being beaten down the street.

Her mother sighed. "Summer is over."

Josie drew closer to her, with a sense of consolation. Her mother's dark plait was as warm as her arm, and she tugged at it. In the coming of these glittering flashes and the cries and the calling voices of the equinox, summer was turning into the past. The long ago . . .

"What is the equinox?" she asked.

Her father made an explanation. "A seasonal change, you see, Josie—like the storm we had in winter. You remember that."

"No, sir," she said. She clung to her mother.

"She couldn't remember it next morning," said her mother, and looked at Will, who slept up against his father with his hands in small fists.

"You mustn't be frightened, Josie," said her father again. "You have my word that this is a good strong house." He had built it before she was born. But in the equinox Josie stayed with her mother, though the lightning stamped the pattern of her father's dressing gown on the room.

With the pulse of the lightning the wide front window was oftener light than dark, and the persistence of illumination seemed slowly to be waking something that slept longer than Josie had slept, for her trembling body turned under her mother's hand.

"Be still," said her mother. "It's soon over."

They looked at one another, parents and children, as if through a turning wheel of light, while they waited in their various attitudes against the wicker arabesques and the flowered cloth. When the wind rose still higher, both mother and father went all at once silent, Will's eyes lifted open, and all their gazes confronted one another. Then in a single flickering, Will's face was lost in sleep. The house moved softly like a boat that has been stepped into.

Josie lay drifting in the chair, and where she drifted was through the summertime, the way of the past. . . .

It seemed to her that there should have been more time for the monkey-man—for the premonition, the organ coming from the distance, the crisis in the house, "Is there a penny upstairs or down?", the circle of following children, their downcast looks of ecstasy, and for the cold imploring hand of the little monkey.

She woke only to hunt for signs of the fairies, and counted nothing but a footprint smaller than a bird-claw. All of the sand pile went into a castle, and it was a rite to stretch on her stomach and put her mouth to the door. "O my Queen!" and the coolness of the whisper would stir the grains of sand within. Expectant on the floor were spread the sycamore leaves, Will's fur rugs with the paws, head, and tail. "I am thine eternally, my Queen, and will serve thee always and I will be enchanted with thy love forever." It was delicious to close both eyes and wait a length of time. Then, supposing a mocking-bird sang in the tree, "I ask for my first wish, to be made to understand the tongue of birds." They called her back because they had no memory of magic. Even a June-bug, if he were caught and released, would turn into a being, and this was forgotten in the way people summoned one another.

Polishing the dark hall clock as though it was through her tending that the time was brought, the turbaned cook would be singing, "Dere's a Hole in de Bottom of de Sea." "How old will I get to be, Johanna?" she would ask as she ran through the house. "Ninety-eight." "How old is Will going to be?" "Ninety-nine." Then she was out the door. Her bicycle was the golden Princess, the name in a scroll in front. She would take her as early as possible. So as to touch nothing, to make no print on the earliness of the day, she rode with no hands, no feet, touching nowhere but the one place, moving away into the leaves, down the swaying black boards of the dewy alley. They called her back. She hung from and circled in order the four round posts, warm and filled with weight, on the porch. Green arched ferns, like great exhalations, spread from the stands. The porch was deep and wide and painted white with a blue ceiling, and the swing, like three sides of a box, was white too under its long quiet chains. She ran and jumped, secure that the house was theirs and identical with them—the pale smooth house seeming not to yield to any happening, with the dreamlike arch of the roof over the entrance like the curve of their upper lips.

All the children came running and jumping out. She went along chewing nasturtium stems and sucking the honey from four-o'clock flowers, out for whatever figs and pomegranates came to hand. She floated a rose petal dry in her mouth, and sucked on the spirals of honeysuckle and the knobs of purple clover. She wore crowns. She added flower necklaces as the morning passed, then bracelets, and applied transfer-pictures to her forehead and arms and legs—a basket of roses, a windmill, Columbus's ships, ruins of Athens. But always oblivious, off in the shade, the big girls reclined or pressed their flowers in a book, or filled whole baking-powder cans with four-leaf-clovers they found.

And watching it all from the beginning, the morning going by, was the double-house. This worn old house was somehow in disgrace, as if it had been born into it and could not help it. Josie was sorry, and sorry that it looked like a face, with

its wide-apart upper windows, the nose-like partition between the two sagging porches, the chimneys rising in listening points at either side, and
the roof across which the birds sat. It watched, and
by not being what it should have been, the house
was inscrutable. There was always some noise of
disappointment to be heard coming from within
—a sigh, a thud, something dropped. There were
eight children in all that came out of it—all sizes,
and all tow-headed, as if they might in some way
all be kin under that roof, and they had a habit
of arranging themselves in the barren yard in a
little order, like an octave, and staring out across
the street at the rest of the neighborhood—as if to
state, in their rude way, "This is us." Everyone
was cruelly prevented from playing with the children of the double-house, no matter how in their
humility they might change—in the course of the
summer they would change to an entirely new set,
with the movings in and out, though somehow
there were always exactly eight. Cornella, being
nearly grown and being transformed by age, was
not to be counted simply as a forbidden playmate
—yet sometimes, as if she wanted to be just that,
she chased after them, or stood in the middle while
they ran a ring around her.

In the morning was Cornella's time of prepa-
ration. She was forever making ready. Big girls are

usually idle, but Cornella, as occupied as a child, vigorously sunned her hair, or else she had always just washed it and came out busily to dry it. It was bright yellow, wonderfully silky and long, and she would bend her neck and toss her hair over her head before her face like a waterfall. And her hair was as constant a force as a waterfall to Josie, under whose eyes alone it fell. Cornella, Cornella, let down thy hair, and the King's son will come climbing up.

Josie watched her, for there was no one else to see, how she shook it and played with it and presently began to brush it, over and over, out in public. But always through the hiding hair she would be looking out, steadily out, over the street. Josie, who followed her gaze, felt the emptiness of their street too, and could not understand why at such a moment no one could be as pitiful as only the old man driving slowly by in the cart, and no song could be as sad as his song,

"*Milk, milk,*
Buttermilk!
Sweet potatoes—Irish potatoes—green peas—
And buttermilk!"

But Cornella, instead of being moved by this sad moment, in which Josie's love began to go toward her, stamped her foot. She was angry,

angry. To see her then, oppression touched Josie and held her quite still. Called in to dinner before she could understand, she felt a conviction: I will never catch up with her. No matter how old I get, I will never catch up with Cornella. She felt that daring and risking everything went for nothing; she would never take a poison wild strawberry into her mouth again in the hope of finding out the secret and the punishment of the world, for Cornella, whom she might love, had stamped her foot, and had as good as told her, "You will never catch up." All that she ran after in the whole summer world came to life in departure before Josie's eyes and covered her vision with wings. It kept her from eating her dinner to think of all that she had caught or meant to catch before the time was gone—June-bugs in the banana plants to fly before breakfast on a thread, lightning-bugs that left a bitter odor in the palms of the hands, butterflies with their fierce and haughty faces, bees in a jar. A great tempest of droning and flying seemed to have surrounded her as she ran, and she seemed not to have moved without putting her hand out after something that flew ahead. . . .

"There! I thought you were asleep," said her father.

She turned in her chair. The house had stirred.

"Show me their tracks," muttered Will. "Just show me their tracks."

As though the winds were changed back into songs, Josie seemed to hear "Beautiful Ohio" slowly picked out in the key of C down the hot afternoon. That was Cornella. Through the tied-back curtains of parlors the other big girls, with rats in their hair and lace insertions in their white dresses, practiced forever on one worn little waltz, up and down the street, for they took lessons.

"Come spend the day with me." "See who can eat a banana down without coming up to breathe." That was Josie and her best friend, smirking at each other.

They wandered at a trot, under their own parasols. In the vacant field, in the center of summer, was a chinaberry tree, as dark as a cloud in the middle of the day. Its frail flowers or its bitter yellow balls lay trodden always over the whole of the ground. There was a little path that came through the hedge and went its way to this tree, and there was an old low seat built part-way around the trunk, on which was usually lying an abandoned toy of some kind. Here beside the nurses stood the little children, whose level eyes stared at the rosettes on their garters.

"How do you do?"

"How do you do?"

"I remembers you. Where you all think you goin'?"

"We don't have to answer."

They went to the drugstore and treated each other. It was behind the latticed partition. How well she knew its cut-out pasteboard grapes whose color was put on a little to one side. Her elbows slid smoothly out on the cold camp marble that smelled like hyacinths. "You say first." "No, you. First you love me last you hate me." When they were full of sweets it was never too late to take the long way home. They ran through the park and drank from the fountain. Moving slowly as sunlight over the grass were the broad and dusty backs of pigeons. They stopped and made a clover-chain and hung it on a statue. They groveled in the dirt under the bandstand hunting for lost money, but when they found a dead bird with its feathers cool as rain, they ran out in the sun. Old Biddy Felix came to make a speech, he stood up and shouted with no one to listen—"The time flies, the time flies!"—and his arm and hand flew like a bat in the ragged sleeve. Walking the see-saw she held her breath for him. They floated magnolia leaves in the horse trough, themselves taking the part of the wind and waves, and suddenly remembering who they were. They closed in upon the hot tamale man, fixing their frightened eyes on his lantern and on his scars.

Josie never came and she never went without touching the dragon—the Chinese figure in the garden on the corner that in biting held rain water in the cavern of its mouth. And never did it seem so still, so utterly of stone, as when all the children said goodbye as they always did on that corner, and she was left alone with it. Stone dragons opened their mouths and begged to swallow the day, they loved to eat the summer. It was painful to think of even pony-rides gobbled, the way they all went, the children, every one (except from the double-house) crammed into the basket with their heads stuck up like candy-almonds in a treat. She backed all the way home from the dragon.

But she had only to face the double-house in her meditations, and then she could invoke Cornella. Thy name is Corn, and thou art like the ripe corn, beautiful Cornella. And before long the figure of Cornella would be sure to appear. She would dart forth from one old screen door of the double-house, trailed out by the nagging odor of cabbage cooking. She would have just bathed and dressed, for it took her so long, and her bright hair would be done in puffs and curls with a bow behind.

Cornella was not even a daughter in her side of the house, she was only a niece or cousin, there only by the frailest indulgence. She would come

out with this frailty about her, come without a
hat, without anything. Between the double-house
and the next house was the strongest fence that
could be built, and no ball had ever come back
that went over it. It reached all the way out to the
street. So Cornella could never see if anyone might
be coming, unless she came all the way out to the
curb and leaned around the corner of the fence.
Josie knew the way it would happen, and yet it
was like new always. At the opening of the door,
the little towheads would scatter, dash to the
other side of the partition, disappear as if by consent. Then lightly down the steps, down the walk,
Cornella would come, in some kind of secrecy
swaying from side to side, her skirts swinging
round, and the sidewalk echoing smally to her
pumps with the Baby Louis heels. Then, all alone,
Cornella would turn and gaze away down the
street, as if she could see far, far away, in a little
pantomime of hope and apprehension that would
not permit Josie to stir.

But the moment came when without meaning
to she lifted her hand softly, and made a sign to
Cornella. She almost said her name.

And Cornella—what was it she had called back
across the street, the flash of what word, so furious
and yet so frail and thin? It was more furious than
even the stamping of her foot, only a single word.

Josie took her hand down. In a seeking humility she stood there and bore her shame to attend Cornella. Cornella herself would stand still, haughtily still, waiting as if in pride, until a voice old and cracked would call her too, from the upper window, "Cornella, Cornella!" And she would have to turn around and go inside to the old woman, her hair ribbon and her sash in pale bows that sank down in the back.

Then for Josie the sun on her bangs stung, and the pity for ribbons drove her to a wild capering that would end in a tumble.

Will woke up with a yell like a wild Indian.

"Here, let me hold him," said his mother. Her voice had become soft; time had passed. She took Will on her lap.

Josie opened her eyes. The lightning was flowing like the sea, and the cries were like waves at the door. Her parents' faces were made up of hundreds of very still moments.

"Tomahawks!" screamed Will.

"Mother, don't let him—" Josie said uneasily.

"Never mind. You talk in your sleep too," said her mother.

She experienced a kind of shock, a small shock of detachment, like the time in the picture-show when a little blurred moment of the summer's May Festival had been thrown on the screen and there was herself, ribbon in hand, weaving once in and once out, a burning and abandoned look in the flicker of her face as though no one in the world would ever see her.

Her mother's hand stretched to her, but Josie broke away. She lay with her face hidden in the pillow. . . . The summer day became vast and opalescent with twilight. The calming and languid smell of manure came slowly to meet her as she passed through the back gate and went out to the pasture among the mounds of wild roses. "Daisy," she had only to say once, in her quietest voice, for she felt very near to the cow. There she walked, not even eating—Daisy, the small tender Jersey with her soft violet nose, walking and presenting her warm side. Josie bent to lean her forehead against her. Here the tears from her eyes could go rolling down Daisy's shining coarse hairs, and Daisy did not move or speak but held patient, richly compassionate and still. . . .

"You're not frightened any more, are you, Josie?" asked her father.

"No, sir," she said, with her face buried. . . . She thought of the evening, the sunset, the stately game played by the flowering hedge when the vacant field was theirs. "Here comes the duke a-riding, riding, riding . . . What are you riding here for, here for?" while the hard iron sound of the Catholic Church bell tolled at twilight for un-

known people. "The fairest one that I can see
. . . London Bridge is falling down . . . Lady
Moon, Lady Moon, show your shoe . . . I meas-
ure my love to show you . . ." Under the fiery
windows, how small the children were. "Fox in
the morning!—Geese in the evening!—How many
have you got?—More than you can ever catch!"
The children were rose-colored too. Fading, rolling shouts cast long flying shadows behind them,
and to watch them she stood still. Above everything in the misty blue dome of the sky was the
full white moon. So it is, for a true thing, round,
she thought, and where she waited a hand seemed
to reach around and take her under the loose-
hanging hair, and words in her thoughts came
shaped like grapes in her throat. She felt lonely.
She would stop a runner. "Did you know the
moon was round?" "I did. Annie told me last
summer." The game went on. But I must find
out everything about the moon, Josie thought in
the solemnity of evening. The moon and tides. O
moon! O tides! I ask thee. I ask thee. Where dost
thou rise and fall? As if it were this knowledge
which she would allow to enter her heart, for
which she had been keeping room, and as if it
were the moon, known to be round, that would go
floating through her dreams forever and never
leave her, she looked steadily up at the moon. The

moon looked down at her, full with all the lonely time to go.

When night was about to fall, the time came to bring out her most precious possession, the steamboat she had made from a shoe-box. In all boats the full-moon, half-moon, and new moon were cut out of each side for the windows, with tissue-paper through which shone the unsteady candle inside. She knew this journey ahead of time as if it were long ago, the hushing noise the boat made being dragged up the brick walk by the string, the leap it had to take across the three-cornered missing place over the big root, the spreading smell of warm wax in the evening, and the re-membered color of the daylight turning. Coming to meet the boat was another boat, shining and gliding as if by itself.

Children greeted each other dreamily at twi-light.

"Choo-choo!"

"Choo-choo!"

And something made her turn after that and see how Cornella stood and looked across at them, all dressed in gauze, looking as if the street were a river flowing along between, and she did not speak at all. Josie understood: she *could* not. It seemed to her as she guided her warm boat under the brightening moon that Cornella would have turned into a tree if she could, there in the front yard of the double-house, and that the center of the tree would have to be seen into before her heart was bared, so undaunted and so filled with hope. . . .

"I'll shoot you dead!" screamed Will.

"Hush, hush," said their mother.

Her father held up his hand and said, "Listen."

Then their house was taken to the very breast of the storm.

Josie lay as still as an animal, and in panic thought of the future . . . the sharp day when she would come running out of the field holding the ragged stems of the quick-picked goldenrod and the warm flowers thrust out for a present for somebody. The future was herself bringing presents, the season of gifts. When would the day come when the wind would fall and they would sit in silence on the fountain rim, their play done, and the boys would crack the nuts under their heels? If they would bring the time around once more, she would lose nothing that was given, she would hoard the nuts like a squirrel.

For the first time in her life she thought, might the same wonders never come again? Was each wonder original and alone like the falling star, and when it fell did it bury itself beyond where you hunted it? Should she hope to see it snow twice, and the teacher running again to open the

window, to hold out her black cape to catch it as it
came down, and then going up and down the room
quickly, quickly, to show them the snowflakes? . . .

"Mama, where is my muff that came from Mar-
shall Field's?"

"It's put away, it was your grandmother's present." (But it came from those far fields.) "Are you
dreaming?" Her mother felt of her forehead.

"I want my little muff to hold." She ached for it.
"Mother, give it to me."

"Keep still," said her mother softly.

Her father came over and kissed her, and as if
a new kiss could bring a memory, she remembered
the night. . . . It was that very night. How could
she have forgotten and nearly let go what was clos-
est of all? . . .

The whole way, as they walked slowly after
supper past the houses, and the wet of sprinkled
lawns was rising like a spirit over the streets, the
locusts were filling the evening with their old de-
lirium, the swell that would rise and die away.

In the Chautauqua when they got there, there
was a familiar little cluster of stars beyond the hole
in the top of the tent, but the canvas sides gave off
sighs and stirred, and a knotted rope knocked outside. It was war time where there were grown
people, and the vases across the curtained stage

held little bunches of flags on sticks which drooped and wilted like flowers before their eyes. Josie and Will sat waiting on the limber board in the front row, their feet hanging into the spice-clouds of sawdust. The curtains parted. Waiting with lifted hands was a company with a sign beside them saying "The Trio." All were ladies, one in red, one in white, and one in blue, and after one smile which touched them all at the same instant, like a match struck in their faces, they began to play a piano, a cornet, and a violin.

At first, in the hushed disappointment which filled the Chautauqua tent in beginning moments, the music had been sparse and spare, like a worn hedge through which the hiders can be seen. But then, when hope had waned, there had come a little transition to another key, and the woman with the cornet had stepped forward, raising her instrument.

If morning-glories had come out of the horn instead of those sounds, Josie would not have felt a more astonished delight. She was pierced with pleasure. The sounds that so tremulously came from the striving of the lips were welcome and sweet to her. Between herself and the lifted cornet there was no barrier, there was only the stale, expectant air of the old shelter of the tent. The cornetist was beautiful. There in the flame-like glare that was somehow shadowy, she had come from far away, and the long times of the world seemed to be about her. She was draped heavily in white, shaded with blue, like a Queen, and she stood braced and looking upward like the figure-head on a Viking ship. As the song drew out, Josie could see the slow appearance of a little vein in her cheek. Her closed eyelids seemed almost to whir and yet to rest motionless, like the wings of a humming-bird, when she reached the high note. The breaths she took were fearful, and a little medallion of some kind lifted each time on her breast. Josie listened in mounting care and suspense, as if the performance led in some direction away—as if a destination were being shown her.

And there not far away, with her face all wild, was Cornella, listening too, and still alone. In some alertness Josie turned and looked back for her parents, but they were far back in the crowd; they did not see her, they were not listening. She was let free, and turning back to the cornetist, who was transfixed beneath her instrument, she bent gently forward and closed her hands together over her knees.

"Josie!" whispered Will, prodding her.

"That's my name." But she would not talk to him.

She had come home tired, in a dream. But after the light had been turned out on the sleeping porch, and the kisses of her family were put on her cheek, she had not fallen asleep. She could see out from the high porch that the town was dark, except where beyond the farthest rim of trees the old cotton-seed mill with its fiery smoke-stack and its lights forever seemed an inland boat that waited for the return of the sea. It came over her how the beauty of the world had come with its sign and stridden through their town that night; and it seemed to her that a proclamation had been made in the last high note of the lady trumpeter when her face had become set in its passion, and that after that there would be no more waiting and no more time left for the one who did not take heed and follow. . . .

There was a breaking sound, the first thunder.

"You see!" said her father. He struck his palms together, and it thundered again. "It's over."

"Back to bed, every last one of you," said her mother, as if it had all been something done to tease her, and now her defiance had won. She turned a light on and off.

"Pow!" cried Will, and then toppled into his father's arms, and was carried up the stairs.

From then on there was only the calm steady falling of rain.

Josie was placed in her winter-time bed. They would think her asleep, for they had all kissed one another in a kind of triumph to do for the rest of the night. The rain was a sleeper's sound. She listened for a time to a tapping that came at her window, like a plea from outside. . . . From whom? She could not know. Cornella, sweet summertime, the little black monkey, poor Biddy Felix, the lady with the horn whose lips were parted? Had they after all asked something of her? There, outside, was all that was wild and beloved and estranged, and all that would beckon and leave her, and all that was beautiful. She wanted to follow, and by some metamorphosis she would take them in—all—every one. . . .

The first thing next morning Josie ran outdoors to see what signs the equinox had left. The sun was shining. Will was already out, gruffly exhorting himself, digging in his old hole to China. The double-house across the street looked as if its old age had come upon it at last. Nobody was to be seen at the windows, and not a child was near. The whole façade drooped and gave way in the soft light, like the face of an old woman fallen asleep in church. In all the trees in all the yards the leaves were slowly dropping, one by one, as if in breath after breath.

There at Josie's foot on the porch was something. It was a folded bit of paper, wet and pale and thin, trembling in the air and clinging to the pedestal of the column, as though this were the residue of some great wave that had rolled upon the rock and then receded for another time. It was a fragment of a letter. It was written not properly in ink but in indelible pencil, and so its message had not been washed away as it might have been.

Josie knelt down and took the paper in both hands, and without moving read all that was there. Then she went to her room and put it into her most secret place, the little drawstring bag that held her dancing shoes. The name Cornella was on it, and it said, "O my darling I have waited so long when are you coming for me? Never a day or a night goes by that I do not ask When? When? When?" . . .

THE PURPLE HAT

$\mathscr{I}$T WAS in a bar, a quiet little
hole in the wall. It was four o'clock in the afternoon. Beyond the open door the rain fell, the
heavy color of the sea, in air where the sunlight
was still suspended. Its watery reflection lighted
the room, as a room might have lighted a mouse-
hole. It was in New Orleans.

There was a bartender whose mouth and eyes
curved downward from the divide of his baby-
pink nose, as if he had combed them down, like
his hair; he always just said nothing. The seats
at his bar were black oilcloth knobs, worn and
smooth and as much alike as six pebbles on the
beach, and yet the two customers had chosen very
particularly the knobs they would sit on. They
had come in separately out of the wet, and had
each chosen an end stool, and now sat with the
length of the little bar between them. The bartender obviously did not know either one; he
rested his eyes by closing them. . . .

The fat customer, with a rather affable look about him, said he would have a rye. The unshaven young man with the shaking hands, though he had come in first, only looked fearfully at a spot on the counter before him until the bartender, as if he could hear silent prayer, covered the spot with a drink.

The fat man swallowed, and began at once to look a little cosy and prosperous. He seemed ready to speak, if the moment came. . . .

There was a calm roll of thunder, no more than a shifting of the daily rain clouds over Royal Street.

Then—"Rain or shine," the fat man spoke, "she'll be there."

The bartender stilled his cloth on the bar, as if mopping up made a loud noise, and waited.

"Why, at the Palace of Pleasure," said the fat man. He was really more heavy and solid than he was simply fat.

The bartender leaned forward an inch on his hand.

"The lady will be at the Palace of Pleasure," said the fat man in his drowsy voice. "The lady with the purple hat."

Then the fat man turned on the black knob, put his elbow on the counter, and rested his cheek on his hand, where he could see all the way down the bar. For a moment his eyes seemed dancing there, above one of those hands so short and so plump that you are always counting the fingers . . . really helpless-looking hands for so large a man.

The young man stared back without much curiosity, looking at the affable face much the way you stare out at a little station where your train is passing through. His hand alone found its place on his small glass.

"Oh, the hat she wears is a creation," said the fat man, almost dreamily, yet not taking his eyes from the young man. It was strange that he did not once regard the bartender, who after all had done him the courtesy of asking a polite question or two, or at least the same as asked. "A great and ancient and bedraggled purple hat."

There was another rumble overhead. Here they seemed to inhabit the world that was just beneath the thunder. The fat man let it go by, lifting his little finger like a pianist. Then he went on.

"Sure, she's one of those thousands of middle-aged women who come every day to the Palace, would not be kept away by anything on earth. . . . Most of them are dull enough, drab old creatures, all of them, walking in with their big black purses held wearily by the handles like suitcases packed for a trip. No one has ever been able to find out how all these old creatures can leave their lives at home like that to gamble . . . what their hus-

bands think . . . who keeps the house in order
. . . who pays. . . . At any rate, she is one like
the rest, except for the hat, and except for the
young man that always meets her there, from year
to year. . . . And I think she is a ghost."

"Ghost!" said the bartender—noncommittally,
just as he might repeat an order.

"For this reason," said the fat man.

A reminiscent tone came into his voice which
seemed to put the silent thin young man on his
guard. He made the beginning of a gesture toward
the bottle. The bartender was already filling his
glass.

"In thirty years she has not changed," said the
fat man. "Neither has she changed her hat. Dear
God, how the moths must have hungered for that
hat. But she has kept it in full bloom on her head,
that monstrosity—purple, too, as if she were beautiful in the bargain. She has not aged, but she
keeps her middle-age. The young man, on the
other hand, must change—I'm sure he's not always the same young man. For thirty years," he
said, "she's met a young man at the dice table
every afternoon, rain or shine, at five o'clock, and
gambles till midnight and tells him goodbye, and
still it looks to be always the same young man—
always young, but a little stale, a little tired . . .
the smudge of a sideburn. . . . She finds them,
she does. She picks them. Where I don't know,

unless New Orleans, as I've always had a guess, is the birthplace of ready-made victims."

"Who are you?" asked the young man. It was the sort of idle voice in which the greatest wildness sometimes speaks out at last in a quiet bar.

"In the Palace of Pleasure there is a little cat-walk along beneath the dome," said the fat man. His rather small, mournful lips, such as big men often have, now parted in a vague smile. "I am the man whose eyes look out over the gambling room. I am the armed man that everyone knows to be watching, at all they do. I don't believe my position is dignified by a title." Nevertheless, he looked rather pleased. "I have watched her every day for thirty years and I think she is a ghost. I have seen her murdered twice," said the fat man.

The bartender's enormous sad black eyebrows raised, like hoods on baby-carriages, and showed his round eyes.

The fat man lifted his other fat little hand and studied, or rather showed off, a ruby ring that he wore on his little finger. "That carpet, if you have ever been there, in the Palace of Pleasure, is red, but from up above, it changes and gives off light between the worn criss-crossing of the aisles like the facets of a well-cut ruby," he said, speaking in a declarative manner as if he had been waiting for a chance to deliver this enviable comparison. "The tables and chandeliers are far down below me, points in its interior. . . . Life in the ruby. And yet somehow all that people do is clear and lucid and authentic there, as if it were magnified in the red lens, not made smaller. I can see everything in the world from my catwalk. You mustn't think I brag. . . ." He looked all at once from his ring straight at the young man's face, which was as drained and white as ever, expressionless, with a thin drop of whisky running down his cheek where he had blundered with his glass.

"I have seen this old and disgusting creature in her purple hat every night, quite plainly, for thirty years, and to my belief she has been murdered twice. I suppose it will take the third time." He himself smoothly tossed down a drink.

The bartender leaned over and filled the young man's glass.

"It's within the week, within the month, that she comes back. Once she was shot point-blank— that was the first time. The young man was hotheaded then. I saw her carried out bleeding from the face. We hush those things, you know, at the Palace. There are no signs afterwards, no trouble. . . . The soft red carpet . . . Within the month she was back—with her young man meeting her at the table just after five."

The bartender put his head to one side.

"The only good of shooting her was, it made a brief period of peace there," said the fat man. "I wouldn't scoff, if I were you." He did seem the least bit fretted by that kind of interruption.

"The second time took into account the hat," he went on. "And I do think her young man was on his way toward the right idea that time, the secret. I think he had learned something. Or he wanted it all kept more quiet, or he was a new one. . . ." He looked at the young man at the other end of the bar with a patient, compassionate expression, or it may have been the inevitably tender contour of his round cheeks. "It is time that I told you about the hat. It is quite a hat. A great, wide, deep hat such as has no fashion and never knew there was fashion and change. It serves her to come out in winter and summer. Those are old plush flowers that trim it—roses? Poppies? A man wouldn't know easily. And you would never know if you only met her wearing the hat that a little glass vial with a plunger helps decorate the crown. You would have to see it from above. . . . Or you would need to be the young man sitting beside her at the gambling table when, at some point in the evening, she takes the hat off and lays it carefully in her lap, under the table. . . . Then you might notice the little vial, and be attracted to it and wish to take it out and examine it at your pleasure off in the washroom—to admire the handle, for instance, which is red glass, like the petal of an artificial flower."

The bartender suddenly lifted his hand to his mouth as if it held a glass, and yawned into it. The thin young man hit the counter faintly with his tumbler.

"She does more than just that, though," said the fat man with a little annoyance in his soft voice. "Perhaps I haven't explained that she is a lover, too, or did you know that she would be? It is hard to make it clear to a man who has never been out to the Palace of Pleasure, but only serves drinks all day behind a bar. You see . . ." And now, lowering his voice a little, he deliberately turned from the young man and would not look at him any more. But the young man looked at him, without lifting his drink—as if there were something hypnotic and irresistible even about his side face with the round, hiding cheek.

"Try to imagine," the fat man was saying gently to the bartender, who looked back at him. "At some point in the evening she always takes off the purple hat. Usually it is very late . . . when it is almost time for her to go. The young man who has come to the rendezvous watches her until she removes it, watches her hungrily. Is it in order to see her hair? Well, most ghosts that are lovers, and lovers that are ghosts, have the long thick black hair that you would expect, and hers is no exception to the rule. It is pinned up, of course—in her straggly vague way. But the young man doesn't look at it after all. He is enamoured of her hat—her ancient, battered, outrageous hat with the awful plush flowers. She lays it down below the level of the table there, on her shabby old lap, and he caresses it. . . . Well, I suppose in this town there are stranger forms of love than that, and who are any of us to say what ways people may not find to love? She herself, you know, seems perfectly satisfied with it. And yet she must not be satisfied, being a ghost. . . . Does it matter how she seeks her desire? I am sure she speaks to him, in a sort of purr, the purr that is used for talking in that room, and the young man does not know what she seeks of him, and she is leading him on, all the time. What does she say? I do not know. But believe me . . . she leads him on. . . ."

The bartender leaned on one hand. He had an oddly cheerful look by this time, as if with strange and sad things to come his way his outlook became more vivacious.

"To look at, she has a large-sized head," said the fat man, pushing his lip with his short finger. "Well, it is more that her face spreads over such a wide area. Like the moon's. . . . Much as I have studied her, I can only say that all her features seem to have moved further apart from each other—expanded, if you see what I mean." He brought his hands together and parted them.

The bartender leaned over closer, staring at the fat man's face interestedly.

"But I can never finish telling you about the hat!" the fat man cried, and there was a little sigh somewhere in the room, very young, like a child's. "Of course, to balance the weight of the attractive little plunger, there is an object to match on the other side of this marvelous old hat—a jeweled hatpin, no less. Of course the pin is there to keep the hat safe! Each time she takes off the hat, she has first to remove the hatpin. You can see her do it every night of the world. It comes out a regular little flashing needle, ten or twelve inches long, and after she has taken the hat off, she sticks the pin back through."

The bartender pursed his lips.

"What about the second time she was murdered? Have you wondered how that was done?" The fat man turned back to face the young fellow, whose feet drove about beneath the stool. "The young lover had learned something, or come to some conclusion, you see," he said. "It was obvious all the time, of course, that by spinning the brim ever so easily as it rested on the lady's not over-sensitive old knees, it would be possible to remove the *opposite* ornament. There was not the slightest fuss or outcry when the pin entered between the ribs and pierced the heart. No one saw it done . . . except for me, naturally—I had been watching for it, more or less. The old creature, who had been winning at that, simply folded all softly in on herself, like a circus tent being taken down after the show, if you've ever seen the sight. I saw her carried out again. It takes three big boys every time, she is so heavy, and one of them always has the presence of mind to cover her piously with her old purple hat for the occasion."

The bartender shut his eyes distastefully.

"If you had ever been to the Palace of Pleasure, you'd know it all went completely as usual—people at the tables never turn around," said the fat man.

The bartender ran his hand down the side of his sad smooth hair.

"The trouble lies, you see," said the fat man, "with the young lover. You are he, let us say. . . ." But he turned from the drinking young man, and it was the bartender who was asked to be the lover for the moment. "After a certain length of time goes by, and love has blossomed, and the hat, the purple hat, is thrilling to the touch of your hand —you can no longer be sure about the little vial. There in privacy you may find it to be empty. It

is her coquettishness, you see. She leads you on.
You are never to know whether . . ."

The chimes of St. Louis Cathedral went som-
nambulantly through the air. It was five o'clock.
The young man had risen somehow to his feet.
He moved out of the bar and disappeared in the
rain of the alley. On the floor where his feet had
been were old cigarette stubs that had been kicked
and raked into a little circle—a rosette, a clock,
a game wheel, or something. . . .

The bartender put a cork in the bottle.

"I have to go myself," said the fat man.

Once more the bartender raised his great
hooded brows. For a moment their eyes met. The
fat man pulled out an enormous roll of worn
bills. He paid in full for all drinks and added a
nice tip.

"Up on the catwalk you get the feeling now
and then that you could put out your finger and
make a change in the universe." His great shoulders lifted.

The bartender, with his hands full of cash,
leaned confidentially over the bar. "Is she a real
ghost?" he asked, in a real whisper.

There was a pause, which the thunder filled.

"I'll let you know tomorrow," said the fat man.

Then he too was gone.

LIVVIE

*S*OLOMON carried Livvie twenty-one miles away from her home when he married her. He carried her away up on the Old Natchez Trace into the deep country to live in his house. She was sixteen—an only girl, then. Once people said he thought nobody would ever come along there. He told her himself that it had been a long time, and a day she did not know about, since that road was a traveled road with *people* coming and going. He was good to her, but he kept her in the house. She had not thought that she could not get back. Where she came from, people said an old man did not want anybody in the world to ever find his wife, for fear they would steal her back from him. Solomon asked her before he took her, "Would she be happy?"—very dignified, for he was a colored man that owned his land and had it written down in the courthouse; and she said, "Yes, sir," since he was an old man and she was young and just listened and answered. He asked

her, if she was choosing winter, would she pine
for spring, and she said, "No indeed." Whatever
she said, always, was because he was an old man
. . . while nine years went by. All the time, he
got old, and he got so old he gave out. At last he
slept the whole day in bed, and she was young
still.

It was a nice house, inside and outside both. In
the first place, it had three rooms. The front room
was papered in holly paper, with green palmettos
from the swamp spaced at careful intervals over
the walls. There was fresh newspaper cut with
fancy borders on the mantel-shelf, on which were
propped photographs of old or very young men
printed in faint yellow—Solomon's people. Solomon had a houseful of furniture. There was a
double settee, a tall scrolled rocker and an organ
in the front room, all around a three-legged table
with a pink marble top, on which was set a lamp
with three gold feet, besides a jelly glass with
pretty hen feathers in it. Behind the front room,
the other room had the bright iron bed with the
polished knobs like a throne, in which Solomon
slept all day. There were snow-white curtains of
wiry lace at the window, and a lace bed-spread
belonged on the bed. But what old Solomon slept
so sound under was a big feather-stitched piece-
quilt in the pattern "Trip Around the World,"
which had twenty-one different colors, four hun-

dred and forty pieces, and a thousand yards of thread, and that was what Solomon's mother made in her life and old age. There was a table holding the Bible, and a trunk with a key. On the wall were two calendars, and a diploma from somewhere in Solomon's family, and under that Livvie's one possession was nailed, a picture of the little white baby of the family she worked for, back in Natchez before she was married. Going through that room and on to the kitchen, there was a big wood stove and a big round table always with a wet top and with the knives and forks in one jelly glass and the spoons in another, and a cut-glass vinegar bottle between, and going out from those, many shallow dishes of pickled peaches, fig preserves, watermelon pickles and blackberry jam always sitting there. The churn sat in the sun, the doors of the safe were always both shut, and there were four baited mouse-traps in the kitchen, one in every corner.

The outside of Solomon's house looked nice. It was not painted, but across the porch was an even balance. On each side there was one easy chair with high springs, looking out, and a fern basket hanging over it from the ceiling, and a dishpan of zinnia seedlings growing at its foot on the floor. By the door was a plow-wheel, just a pretty iron circle, nailed up on one wall and a square mirror on the other, a turquoise-blue comb stuck up in the frame, with the wash stand beneath it. On the door was a wooden knob with a pearl in the end, and Solomon's black hat hung on that, if he was in the house.

Out front was a clean dirt yard with every vestige of grass patiently uprooted and the ground scarred in deep whorls from the strike of Livvie's broom. Rose bushes with tiny blood-red roses blooming every month grew in threes on either side of the steps. On one side was a peach tree, on the other a pomegranate. Then coming around up the path from the deep cut of the Natchez Trace below was a line of bare crape-myrtle trees with every branch of them ending in a colored bottle, green or blue. There was no word that fell from Solomon's lips to say what they were for, but Livvie knew that there could be a spell put in trees, and she was familiar from the time she was born with the way bottle trees kept evil spirits from coming into the house—by luring them inside the colored bottles, where they cannot get out again. Solomon had made the bottle trees with his own hands over the nine years, in labor amounting to about a tree a year, and without a sign that he had any uneasiness in his heart, for he took as much pride in his precautions against spirits coming in the house as he took in the house, and sometimes in the sun the bottle trees looked prettier than the house did.

It was a nice house. It was in a place where the days would go by and surprise anyone that they were over. The lamplight and the firelight would shine out the door after dark, over the still and breathing country, lighting the roses and the bottle trees, and all was quiet there.

But there was nobody, nobody at all, not even a white person. And if there had been anybody, Solomon would not have let Livvie look at them, just as he would not let her look at a field hand, or a field hand look at her. There was no house near, except for the cabins of the tenants that were forbidden to her, and there was no house as far as she had been, stealing away down the still, deep Trace. She felt as if she waded a river when she went, for the dead leaves on the ground reached as high as her knees, and when she was all scratched and bleeding she said it was not like a road that went anywhere. One day, climbing up the high bank, she had found a graveyard without a church, with ribbon-grass growing about the foot of an angel (she had climbed up because she thought she saw angel wings), and in the sun, trees shining like burning flames through the great caterpillar nets which enclosed them. Scarey thistles stood looking like the prophets in the Bible in Solomon's house. Indian paint brushes grew over her head, and the mourning dove made the only sound in the world. Oh for a stirring of the leaves, and a breaking of the nets! But not by a ghost, prayed Livvie, jumping down the bank. After Solomon took to his bed, she never went out, except one more time.

Livvie knew she made a nice girl to wait on anybody. She fixed things to eat on a tray like a surprise. She could keep from singing when she ironed, and to sit by a bed and fan away the flies, she could be so still she could not hear herself breathe. She could clean up the house and never drop a thing, and wash the dishes without a sound, and she would step outside to churn, for churning sounded too sad to her, like sobbing, and if it made her home-sick and not Solomon, she did not think of that.

But Solomon scarcely opened his eyes to see her, and scarcely tasted his food. He was not sick or paralyzed or in any pain that he mentioned, but he was surely wearing out in the body, and no matter what nice hot thing Livvie would bring him to taste, he would only look at it now, as if he were past seeing how he could add anything more to himself. Before she could beg him, he would go fast asleep. She could not surprise him any more, if he would not taste, and she was afraid that he was never in the world going to taste another thing she brought him—and so how could he last?

✦

But one morning it was breakfast time and she cooked his eggs and grits, carried them in on a tray, and called his name. He was sound asleep. He lay in a dignified way with his watch beside him, on his back in the middle of the bed. One hand drew the quilt up high, though it was the first day of spring. Through the white lace curtains a little puffy wind was blowing as if it came from round cheeks. All night the frogs had sung out in the swamp, like a commotion in the room, and he had not stirred, though she lay wide awake and saying "Shh, frogs!" for fear he would mind them.

He looked as if he would like to sleep a little longer, and so she put back the tray and waited a little. When she tiptoed and stayed so quiet, she surrounded herself with a little reverie, and sometimes it seemed to her when she was so stealthy that the quiet she kept was for a sleeping baby, and that she had a baby and was its mother. When she stood at Solomon's bed and looked down at him, she would be thinking, "He sleeps so well," and she would hate to wake him up. And in some other way, too, she was afraid to wake him up because even in his sleep he seemed to be such a strict man.

Of course, nailed to the wall over the bed— only she would forget who it was—there was a picture of him when he was young. Then he had

a fan of hair over his forehead like a king's crown.
Now his hair lay down on his head, the spring
had gone out of it. Solomon had a lightish face,
with eyebrows scattered but rugged, the way
privet grows, strong eyes, with second sight, a
strict mouth, and a little gold smile. This was the
way he looked in his clothes, but in bed in the
daytime he looked like a different and smaller
man, even when he was wide awake, and holding
the Bible. He looked like somebody kin to himself. And then sometimes when he lay in sleep
and she stood fanning the flies away, and the light
came in, his face was like new, so smooth and
clear that it was like a glass of jelly held to the
window, and she could almost look through his
forehead and see what he thought.

She fanned him and at length he opened his
eyes and spoke her name, but he would not taste
the nice eggs she had kept warm under a pan.

Back in the kitchen she ate heartily, his breakfast and hers, and looked out the open door at
what went on. The whole day, and the whole
night before, she had felt the stir of spring close
to her. It was as present in the house as a young
man would be. The moon was in the last quarter
and outside they were turning the sod and plant-
ing peas and beans. Up and down the red fields,
over which smoke from the brush-burning hung
showing like a little skirt of sky, a white horse

and a white mule pulled the plow. At intervals
hoarse shouts came through the air and roused
her as if she dozed neglectfully in the shade, and
they were telling her, "Jump up!" She could see
how over each ribbon of field were moving men
and girls, on foot and mounted on mules, with
hats set on their heads and bright with tall hoes
and forks as if they carried streamers on them
and were going to some place on a journey—and
how as if at a signal now and then they would
all start at once shouting, hollering, cajoling, calling and answering back, running, being leaped on
and breaking away, flinging to earth with a shout
and lying motionless in the trance of twelve
o'clock. The old women came out of the cabins
and brought them the food they had ready for
them, and then all worked together, spread evenly
out. The little children came too, like a bouncing
stream overflowing the fields, and set upon the
men, the women, the dogs, the rushing birds, and
the wave-like rows of earth, their little voices almost too high to be heard. In the middle distance
like some white and gold towers were the hay-
stacks, with black cows coming around to eat their
edges. High above everything, the wheel of fields,
house, and cabins, and the deep road surrounding
like a moat to keep them in, was the turning sky,
blue with long, far-flung white mare's-tail clouds,
serene and still as high flames. And sound asleep

while all this went around him that was his, Solomon was like a little still spot in the middle.

Even in the house the earth was sweet to breathe. Solomon had never let Livvie go any farther than the chicken house and the well. But what if she would walk now into the heart of the fields and take a hoe and work until she fell stretched out and drenched with her efforts, like other girls, and laid her cheek against the laid-open earth, and shamed the old man with her humbleness and delight? To shame him! A cruel wish could come in uninvited and so fast while she looked out the back door. She washed the dishes and scrubbed the table. She could hear the cries of the little lambs. Her mother, that she had not seen since her wedding day, had said one time, "I rather a man be anything, than a woman be mean."

So all morning she kept tasting the chicken broth on the stove, and when it was right she poured off a nice cup-ful. She carried it in to Solomon, and there he lay having a dream. Now what did he dream about? For she saw him sigh gently as if not to disturb some whole thing he held round in his mind, like a fresh egg. So even an old man dreamed about something pretty. Did he dream of her, while his eyes were shut and sunken, and his small hand with the wedding ring curled close in sleep around the quilt? He might

be dreaming of what time it was, for even through
his sleep he kept track of it like a clock, and knew
how much of it went by, and waked up knowing
where the hands were even before he consulted
the silver watch that he never let go. He would
sleep with the watch in his palm, and even holding it to his cheek like a child that loves a play-
thing. Or he might dream of journeys and travels
on a steamboat to Natchez. Yet she thought he
dreamed of her; but even while she scrutinized
him, the rods of the foot of the bed seemed to rise
up like a rail fence between them, and she could
see that people never could be sure of anything
as long as one of them was asleep and the other
awake. To look at him dreaming of her when he
might be going to die frightened her a little, as
if he might carry her with him that way, and she
wanted to run out of the room. She took hold of
the bed and held on, and Solomon opened his eyes
and called her name, but he did not want anything. He would not taste the good broth.

Just a little after that, as she was taking up the
ashes in the front room for the last time in the
year, she heard a sound. It was somebody coming.
She pulled the curtains together and looked
through the slit.
Coming up the path under the bottle trees was
a white lady. At first she looked young, but then

she looked old. Marvelous to see, a little car stood steaming like a kettle out in the field-track—it had come without a road.

Livvie stood listening to the long, repeated knockings at the door, and after a while she opened it just a little. The lady came in through the crack, though she was more than middle-sized and wore a big hat.

"My name is Miss Baby Marie," she said.

Livvie gazed respectfully at the lady and at the little suitcase she was holding close to her by the handle until the proper moment. The lady's eyes were running over the room, from palmetto to palmetto, but she was saying, "I live at home . . . out from Natchez . . . and get out and show these pretty cosmetic things to the white people and the colored people both . . . all around . . . years and years. . . . Both shades of powder and rouge. . . . It's the kind of work a girl can do and not go clear 'way from home . . ." And the harder she looked, the more she talked. Suddenly she turned up her nose and said, "It is not Christian or sanitary to put feathers in a vase," and then she took a gold key out of the front of her dress and began unlocking the locks on her suitcase. Her face drew the light, the way it was covered with intense white and red, with a little patty-cake of white between the wrinkles by her upper lip. Little red tassels of hair bobbed under the rusty wires of her picture-hat, as with an air of triumph and secrecy she now drew open her little suitcase and brought out bottle after bottle and jar after jar, which she put down on the table, the mantel-piece, the settee, and the organ.

"Did you ever see so many cosmetics in your life?" cried Miss Baby Marie.

"No'm," Livvie tried to say, but the cat had her tongue.

"Have you ever applied cosmetics?" asked Miss Baby Marie next.

"No'm," Livvie tried to say.

"Then look!" she said, and pulling out the last thing of all, "Try this!" she said. And in her hand was unclenched a golden lipstick which popped open like magic. A fragrance came out of it like incense, and Livvie cried out suddenly, "China-berry flowers!"

Her hand took the lipstick, and in an instant she was carried away in the air through the spring, and looking down with a half-drowsy smile from a purple cloud she saw from above a chinaberry tree, dark and smooth and neatly leaved, neat as a guinea hen in the dooryard, and there was her home that she had left. On one side of the tree was her mama holding up her heavy apron, and she could see it was loaded with ripe figs, and on the other side was her papa holding a fish-pole over the pond, and she could see it transparently, the little clear fishes swimming up to the brim.

"Oh, no, not chinaberry flowers—secret ingredients," said Miss Baby Marie. "My cosmetics have secret ingredients—not chinaberry flowers."

"It's purple," Livvie breathed, and Miss Baby Marie said, "Use it freely. Rub it on."

Livvie tiptoed out to the wash stand on the front porch and before the mirror put the paint on her mouth. In the wavery surface her face danced before her like a flame. Miss Baby Marie followed her out, took a look at what she had done, and said, "That's it."

Livvie tried to say "Thank you" without moving her parted lips where the paint lay so new.

By now Miss Baby Marie stood behind Livvie and looked in the mirror over her shoulder, twisting up the tassels of her hair. "The lipstick I can let you have for only two dollars," she said, close to her neck.

"Lady, but I don't have no money, never did have," said Livvie.

"Oh, but you don't pay the first time. I make another trip, that's the way I do. I come back again—later."

"Oh," said Livvie, pretending she understood everything so as to please the lady.

"But if you don't take it now, this may be the last time I'll call at your house," said Miss Baby Marie sharply. "It's far away from anywhere, I'll tell you that. You don't live close to anywhere."

"Yes'm. My husband, he keep the *money*," said Livvie, trembling. "He is strict as he can be. He don't know *you* walk in here—Miss Baby Marie!"

"Where is he?"

"Right now, he in yonder sound asleep, an old man. I wouldn't ever ask him for anything."

Miss Baby Marie took back the lipstick and packed it up. She gathered up the jars for both black and white and got them all inside the suitcase, with the same little fuss of triumph with which she had brought them out. She started away.

"Goodbye," she said, making herself look grand from the back, but at the last minute she turned around in the door. Her old hat wobbled as she whispered, "Let me see your husband."

Livvie obediently went on tiptoe and opened the door to the other room. Miss Baby Marie came behind her and rose on her toes and looked in.

"My, what a little tiny old, old man!" she whispered, clasping her hands and shaking her head over them. "What a beautiful quilt! What a tiny old, old man!"

"He can sleep like that all day," whispered Livvie proudly.

They looked at him awhile so fast asleep, and

then all at once they looked at each other. Somehow that was as if they had a secret, for he had never stirred. Livvie then politely, but all at once, closed the door.

"Well! I'd certainly like to leave you with a lipstick!" said Miss Baby Marie vivaciously. She smiled in the door.

"Lady, but I told you I don't have no money, and never did have."

"And never will?" In the air and all around, like a bright halo around the white lady's nodding head, it was a true spring day.

"Would you take eggs, lady?" asked Livvie softly.

"No, I have plenty of eggs—plenty," said Miss Baby Marie.

"I still don't have no money," said Livvie, and Miss Baby Marie took her suitcase and went on somewhere else.

Livvie stood watching her go, and all the time she felt her heart beating in her left side. She touched the place with her hand. It seemed as if her heart beat and her whole face flamed from the pulsing color of her lips. She went to sit by Solomon and when he opened his eyes he could not see a change in her. "He's fixin' to die," she said inside. That was the secret. That was when she went out of the house for a little breath of air.

She went down the path and down the Natchez
Trace a way, and she did not know how far she
had gone, but it was not far, when she saw a sight.
It was a man, looking like a vision—she standing
on one side of the Old Natchez Trace and he
standing on the other.

As soon as this man caught sight of her, he began to look himself over. Starting at the bottom
with his pointed shoes, he began to look up, lifting his peg-top pants the higher to see fully his
bright socks. His coat long and wide and leaf-
green he opened like doors to see his high-up
tawny pants and his pants he smoothed downward
from the points of his collar, and he wore a luminous baby-pink satin shirt. At the end, he reached
gently above his wide platter-shaped round hat,
the color of a plum, and one finger touched at the
feather, emerald green, blowing in the spring
winds.

No matter how she looked, she could never
look so fine as he did, and she was not sorry for
that, she was pleased.

He took three jumps, one down and two up,
and was by her side.

"My name is Cash," he said.

He had a guinea pig in his pocket. They began
to walk along. She stared on and on at him, as if
he were doing some daring spectacular thing, instead of just walking beside her. It was not simply

the city way he was dressed that made her look
at him and see hope in its insolence looking back.
It was not only the way he moved along kicking
the flowers as if he could break through everything in the way and destroy anything in the
world, that made her eyes grow bright. It might
be, if he had not appeared the way he did appear
that day she would never have looked so closely
at him, but the time people come makes a difference.

They walked through the still leaves of the
Natchez Trace, the light and the shade falling
through trees about them, the white irises shining
like candles on the banks and the new ferns shining like green stars up in the oak branches. They
came out at Solomon's house, bottle trees and all.
Livvie stopped and hung her head.

Cash began whistling a little tune. She did not
know what it was, but she had heard it before
from a distance, and she had a revelation. Cash
was a field hand. He was a transformed field hand.
Cash belonged to Solomon. But he had stepped
out of his overalls into this. There in front of
Solomon's house he laughed. He had a round
head, a round face, all of him was young, and he
flung his head up, rolled it against the mare's-tail
sky in his round hat, and he could laugh just to
see Solomon's house sitting there. Livvie looked at
it, and there was Solomon's black hat hanging on

the peg on the front door, the blackest thing in the world.

"I been to Natchez," Cash said, wagging his head around against the sky. "*I* taken a trip, *I* ready for Easter!"

How was it possible to look so fine before the harvest? Cash must have stolen the money, stolen it from Solomon. He stood in the path and lifted his spread hand high and brought it down again and again in his laughter. He kicked up his heels. A little chill went through her. It was as if Cash was bringing that strong hand down to beat a drum or to rain blows upon a man, such an abandon and menace were in his laugh. Frowning, she went closer to him and his swinging arm drew her in at once and the fright was crushed from her body, as a little match-flame might be smothered out by what it lighted. She gathered the folds of his coat behind him and fastened her red lips to his mouth, and she was dazzled by herself then, the way he had been dazzled at himself to begin with.

In that instant she felt something that could not be told—that Solomon's death was at hand, that he was the same to her as if he were dead now. She cried out, and uttering little cries turned and ran for the house.

At once Cash was coming, following after, he was running behind her. He came close, and half-

way up the path he laughed and passed her. He
even picked up a stone and sailed it into the bottle
trees. She put her hands over her head, and sounds
clattered through the bottle trees like cries of
outrage. Cash stamped and plunged zigzag up the
front steps and in at the door.

When she got there, he had stuck his hands in
his pockets and was turning slowly about in the
front room. The little guinea pig peeped out.
Around Cash, the pinned-up palmettos looked as
if a lazy green monkey had walked up and down
and around the walls leaving green prints of his
hands and feet.

She got through the room and his hands were
still in his pockets, and she fell upon the closed
door to the other room and pushed it open. She
ran to Solomon's bed, calling "Solomon! Solomon!" The little shape of the old man never
moved at all, wrapped under the quilt as if it
were winter still.

"Solomon!" She pulled the quilt away, but
there was another one under that, and she fell on
her knees beside him. He made no sound except a
sigh, and then she could hear in the silence the
light springy steps of Cash walking and walking in
the front room, and the ticking of Solomon's silver
watch, which came from the bed. Old Solomon
was far away in his sleep, his face looked small, re-

lentless, and devout, as if he were walking somewhere where she could imagine the snow falling.

Then there was a noise like a hoof pawing the
floor, and the door gave a creak, and Cash appeared beside her. When she looked up, Cash's
face was so black it was bright, and so bright and
bare of pity that it looked sweet to her. She stood
up and held up her head. Cash was so powerful
that his presence gave her strength even when she
did not need any.

Under their eyes Solomon slept. People's faces
tell of things and places not known to the one
who looks at them while they sleep, and while
Solomon slept under the eyes of Livvie and Cash
his face told them like a mythical story that all his
life he had built, little scrap by little scrap, respect. A beetle could not have been more labori-
ous or more ingenious in the task of its destiny.
When Solomon was young, as he was in his picture overhead, it was the infinite thing with him,
and he could see no end to the respect he would
contrive and keep in a house. He had built a
lonely house, the way he would make a cage, but
it grew to be the same with him as a great monu-
mental pyramid and sometimes in his absorption
of getting it erected he was like the builder-slaves
of Egypt who forgot or never knew the origin and
meaning of the thing to which they gave all the

strength of their bodies and used up all their days. Livvie and Cash could see that as a man might rest from a life-labor he lay in his bed, and they could hear how, wrapped in his quilt, he sighed to himself comfortably in sleep, while in his dreams he might have been an ant, a beetle, a bird, an Egyptian, assembling and carrying on his back and building with his hands, or he might have been an old man of India or a swaddled baby, about to smile and brush all away.

Then without warning old Solomon's eyes flew wide open under the hedge-like brows. He was wide awake.

And instantly Cash raised his quick arm. A radiant sweat stood on his temples. But he did not bring his arm down—it stayed in the air, as if something might have taken hold.

It was not Livvie—she did not move. As if something said "Wait," she stood waiting. Even while her eyes burned under motionless lids, her lips parted in a stiff grimace, and with her arms stiff at her sides she stood above the prone old man and the panting young one, erect and apart.

Movement when it came came in Solomon's face. It was an old and strict face, a frail face, but behind it, like a covered light, came an animation that could play hide and seek, that would dart and escape, had always escaped. The mystery flickered

in him, and invited from his eyes. It was that very
mystery that Cash with his quick arm would have
to strike, and that Livvie could not weep for. But
Cash only stood holding his arm in the air, when
the gentlest flick of his great strength, almost a
puff of his breath, would have been enough, if he
had known how to give it, to send the old man
over the obstruction that kept him away from
death.

If it could not be that the tiny illumination in
the fragile and ancient face caused a crisis, a mystery in the room that would not permit a blow to
fall, at least it was certain that Cash, throbbing in
his Easter clothes, felt a pang of shame that the
vigor of a man would come to such an end that he
could not be struck without warning. He took
down his hand and stepped back behind Livvie,
like a round-eyed schoolboy on whose unsuspect-
ing head the dunce cap has been set.

"Young ones can't wait," said Solomon.

Livvie shuddered violently, and then in a gush
of tears she stooped for a glass of water and handed
it to him, but he did not see her.

"So here come the young man Livvie wait for.
Was no prevention. No prevention. Now I lay
eyes on young man and it come to be somebody
I know all the time, and been knowing since he
were born in a cotton patch, and watched grow

up year to year, Cash McCord, growed to size, growed up to come in my house in the end—ragged and barefoot."

Solomon gave a cough of distaste. Then he shut his eyes vigorously, and his lips began to move like a chanter's.

"When Livvie married, her husband were already somebody. He had paid great cost for his land. He spread sycamore leaves over the ground from wagon to door, day he brought her home, so her foot would not have to touch ground. He carried her through his door. Then he growed old and could not lift her, and she were still young."

Livvie's sobs followed his words like a soft melody repeating each thing as he stated it. His lips moved for a little without sound, or she cried too fervently, and unheard he might have been telling his whole life, and then he said, "God forgive Solomon for sins great and small. God forgive Solomon for carrying away too young girl for wife and keeping her away from her people and from all the young people would clamor for her back."

Then he lifted up his right hand toward Livvie where she stood by the bed and offered her his silver watch. He dangled it before her eyes, and she hushed crying; her tears stopped. For a moment the watch could be heard ticking as it always did, precisely in his proud hand. She lifted it away. Then he took hold of the quilt; then he was dead.

Livvie left Solomon dead and went out of the room. Stealthily, nearly without noise, Cash went beside her. He was like a shadow, but his shiny shoes moved over the floor in spangles, and the green downy feather shone like a light in his hat. As they reached the front room, he seized her deftly as a long black cat and dragged her hanging by the waist round and round him, while he turned in a circle, his face bent down to hers. The first moment, she kept one arm and its hand stiff and still, the one that held Solomon's watch. Then the fingers softly let go, all of her was limp, and the watch fell somewhere on the floor. It ticked away in the still room, and all at once there began outside the full song of a bird.

They moved around and around the room and into the brightness of the open door, then he stopped and shook her once. She rested in silence in his trembling arms, unprotesting as a bird on a nest. Outside the redbirds were flying and crisscrossing, the sun was in all the bottles on the prisoned trees, and the young peach was shining in the middle of them with the bursting light of spring.

AT THE LANDING

*T*HE NIGHT that Jenny's grandfather died, he dreamed of high water.

He came in his dream and stood just outside
the door of her room, his little chin that was like
a chicken's clean breastbone tilting upwards.

"It has come," the old man said, and he made a
complaint of it.

Jenny in her bed lay still, waking more still than
in the sleep of a moment before.

"The river has come back. That Floyd came to
tell me. The sun was shining full on the face of
the church, and that Floyd came around it with
his wrist hung with a great long catfish. 'It's coming,' he said. 'It's the river.' Oh, it came then!
Like a head and arm. Like a horse. A mane of
cedar trees tossing over the top. It has borne down,
and it has closed us in. That Floyd was right."

He reached as if to lift an obstacle that he
thought was stretched there—the bar that crossed
the door in her mother's time. It seemed beyond

his strength, she tried to cry out, and he came in through the doorway. The cord and tassel of his brocade robe—for he had put it on—seemed to weigh upon his fragile walking like a chain, and yet it could have been by inexorable will that he wore it, so set were his little steps, in such duty he dragged it.

"Like poor people who have learned to fly at last," he said, walking, dragging, the fine deprecation in his voice, "all the people in The Landing, all kinds and conditions of people, are gliding off and upward to darkness. The little mandolin that my daughter used to play—it's rising like a bubble, and filling with water."

"Grandpa!" cried Jenny, and then she was up and taking her grandfather by his tiny adamant shoulders. It was moonlight. She saw his open eyes. "Wake up, Grandpa!"

"That Floyd's catfish has gone loose and free," he said gently, as if breaking news to someone. "And all of a sudden, my dear—my dears, it took its river life back, and shining so brightly swam through the belfry of the church, and downstream." At that his mouth clamped tight shut.

She held out both arms and he fell trembling against her. With beating heart she carried him through the dark halls to his room and put him down into his bed. He lay there in the moonlight, which moved and crept across him as it would a little fallen withered leaf, and he never moved or spoke any more, but lay softly, as if he were floating, being carried away, drawn by the passing moon; and Jenny's heart beat on and on, sharp as birdsong in the night, under her breast, until day.

Under the shaggy bluff the bottomlands lay in a river of golden haze. The road dropped like a waterfall from the ridge to the town at its foot and came to a grassy end there. It was spring. One slowly moving figure that was a man with a fishing pole passed like a dreamer through the empty street and on through the trackless haze toward the river. The town was still called The Landing. The river had gone, three miles away, beyond sight and smell, beyond the dense trees. It came back only in flood, and boats ran over the houses. Up the light-scattered hill, in the house with the galleries, the old man and his granddaughter had always lived. They were the people least seen in The Landing. The grandfather was too old, and the girl was too shy of the world, and they were both too good—the old ladies said—to come out, and so they stayed inside.

For all her life the shy Jenny could look, if she stayed in the parlor, back and forth between her mother's two paintings, "The Bird Fair" and "The Massacre at Fort Rosalie." Or if she went

in the dining room she could walk around the
table or sit on one after the other of eight needle-
point pieces, each slightly different, which her
mother had worked and sewn to the chairs, or she
could count the plates that stood on their rims in
the closet. In the library she could circle an entirely bare floor and make up a dance to a song
she made up, all silently, or gaze at the backs of
the books without titles—books that had been on
ships and in oxcarts and through fire and water,
and were singed and bleached and swollen and
shrunken, and arranged up high and nearly un-
reachable, like objects of beauty. Wherever she
went she almost touched a prism. The house was
full of prisms. They hung everywhere in the
shadow of the halls and in the sunlight of the
rooms, stirring under the hanging lights, dangling
and circling where they were strung in the window curtains. They gave off the faintest of musical
notes when air stirred in any room or when only
herself passed by, and they touched. It was her way
not to touch them herself, but to let the touch be
magical, a stir of the curtain by the outer air, that
would also make them rainbows. Vases with land-
scapes on them stood in the halls and were reflected endlessly rising in front of her when she
passed quickly between the two mirrors. She
might stop and touch all things, trace their little
pictures with her finger, and put them back again;

it was not forbidden; but her touch that dared not break would have been transparent as a spirit's on the objects. She was calm the way a child is calm, with never the calmness of a spirit. But like distant lightning that silently bathes a whole shimmering sky, one awareness was always trembling about her: one day she would be free to come and go. Nothing now held her in her own room, with the great wardrobe in which she had sometimes longed to hide, and the great box-like canopied bed and the little picture on the wall of her mother with upturned eyes. Jenny could go from room to room, and out at the door. But at the door her grandfather would call her back, with his little murmur.

At sunset the old man and his granddaughter would take their supper in the pavilion on the knoll, that had been a gazebo when the river ran before it. There a little breeze came all the way from the river still. All about the pavilion was an ancient circling thorny rose, like the initial letter in a poetry book. The cook came out and served with exaggerated dignity, as though she scolded in the house. A little picture might be preserved then in all their heads. The old man and the young girl looked across the round table leaf-shadowed under the busy black hands, and smiled by long habit at each other. But her grandfather could not look at her without speculation in his eyes, and the gaze that went so fondly between them held and stretched tight the memory of Jenny's mother. It seemed strange that her mother had been dead now for so many years and yet the wild desire that had torn her seemed still fresh and still a small thing. It was a desire to get to Natchez. People said Natchez was a nice little town on Saturdays with a crowd filling it and moving around.

The grandfather stirred his black coffee and smiled at Jenny. He deprecated raving simply as raving, as a force of Nature and so beneath notice or mention. And yet—even now, too late—if Jenny could plead . . . ! In a heat wave one called the cook to bring a fan, and in his daughter's first raving he rang a bell and told the cook to take her off and sit by her until she had done with it, but in the end she died of it. But Jenny could not plead for her.

Her grandfather, frail as a little bird, would say when it was time to go in. He would rise slowly in the brocade gown he wore to study in, and put his weight, which was the terrifying weight of a claw, on Jenny's arm. Jenny was obedient to her grandfather and would have been obedient to anybody, to a stranger in the street if there could be one. She never performed any act, even a small act, for herself, she would not touch the prisms. It might seem that nothing began in her own heart.

Nothing ever happened, to be seen from the gazebo, except that Billy Floyd went through the town. He was almost unknown, and one to himself. If he came at all, he would come at this time of day. In the long shadows below they could see his figure with the gleaming fish he carried move clear as a candle over the road that he had to himself, and out to the blue distance. In The Landing, every person that moved was watched out of sight, and it made a little pause in every life. And if in each day a moment of hope must come, in Jenny's day the moment was when the rude wild Floyd walked through The Landing carrying the big fish he had caught.

Under the blue sky, skirting the ravine, a half-ring of twenty cedar trees stood leading to the cemetery, their bleached trunks the colors of red and white roses. Jenny, given permission, would walk up there to visit the grave of her mother. The cemetery was a dark shelf above the town, on the site of the old landing place when the ships docked from across the world a hundred years ago, and its brink was marked by an old table-like grave with its top ajar where the woodbine grew. Everywhere there, the hanging moss and the up-thrust stones were in that strange graveyard shade where, by the light they give, the moss seems made of stone, and the stone of moss.

On one of the days, while she sat there on a
stile, Jenny looked across the ravine and there was
Floyd, standing still in a sunny pasture. She could
watch between the grapevines, which hung and
held back like ropes on either side to clear her
view. Floyd had a head of straight light-colored
hair and it hung over his forehead, for he never
was near a comb. He stood facing her in a tall
squared posture of silence and rest, while a rusty-
red horse that belonged to the Lockharts cropped
loudly beside him in the wild-smelling pasture.

It was said by the old ladies that he slept all
morning for he fished all night. Stiff and stern,
Jenny sat there with her feet planted just so on
the step below, in the posture of a child who is
appalled at the stillness and unsurrender of the
still and unsurrendering world.

At last she sighed, and when she took up her
skirt to go, as if she were dreaming she saw Floyd
coming across the pasture toward her. When he
reached the ravine and leaped down into it with
widespread arms as though he jumped into something dangerous, she stood still on the stile to
watch. He moved up near to her now, his feet on
the broken ferns at the spring. The wind whipped
his hair, almost making a noise.

"Go back," she said. She wanted to watch him
a while longer first, before he got to her.

He stopped and looked full at her, his strong

neck bending to one side as if yielding in pleasure to the wind. His arms went down and his fists opened. But for her, his eyes were as bright and unconsumed as stars up in the sky. Then she wanted to catch him and see him close, but not to touch him. He stood watching her, though, as if to prevent it. They were as still and rigid as two mocking-birds that were about to strike their beaks and dance.

She waited, but he smiled, and then knelt and cupped both hands to his face in the spring water. He drank for a long time, while she stood there with her skirt whipping in the wind, and waited on him to see how long he could drink without lifting his face. When he had drunk that much, he went back to the field and threw himself yawning down into the grass. The grass was so deep there that she could see only the one arm flung out in the torn sleeve, straight, sun-blacked and motionless.

The day she watched him in the woods, she felt it come to her dimly that her innocence had left her, since she could watch his. She could only sink down onto the step of the stile, and lay her heavy forehead in her hand. But if innocence had left, she still did not know what was to come. She would wait and see him come awake.

But he slept and slept like the dead, and de-

feated her. She went to her grandfather and left
Floyd sleeping.

Another day, they walked for a little near together, each picking some berry or leaf to hold in
the mouth, on their opposite sides of the little
spring. The pasture, the sun and the grazing horse
were on his side, the graves on hers, and they each
looked across at the other's. The whole world
seemed filled with butterflies. At each step they
took, two black butterflies over the flowers were
whirring just alike, suspended in the air, one
circling the other rhythmically, or both moving
from side to side in a gentle wave-like way, one
above the other. They were blue-black and moving their wings faster than Jenny's eye could follow, always together, like each other's shadows,
beautiful each one with the other. Jenny could
see to start with that no kiss had ever brought love
tenderly enough from mouth to mouth.

Jenny and Floyd stopped and looked for a little
while at all the butterflies and they never touched
each other. When Jenny did touch Floyd, touch
his sleeve, he started.

He went alert in the field like a listening animal. The horse came near and when he touched
it, stood with lifted ears beside him, then broke
away. But over all The Landing there was not a
sound that she could hear. It could only be that
Floyd missed nothing in the world, and could hear

innumerable outward things. He suddenly flung
up his head. She knew he was smiling. And a smile
was always a barrier.

She said his name, for she was so close by. It
was the first time.

He stayed motionless, and she knew that he
lived apart in delight. That could make a strange
glow fall over the field where he was, and the
world go black for her, left behind. She felt terrified, as if at a pitiless thing.

Floyd lifted his foot and stamped on the ground,
and held out his careless arms to catch the horse
he had excited. Then he was jumping on its bare
back and riding into a gallop, shouting to frighten
and amaze whoever listened. She threw herself
down into the grass. Never had she known that
the Lockhart horse could run like that. Floyd went
at a racing speed and he seemed somehow in his
tattered shirt—as she watched from beneath her
arm—to stream with the wind, and he circled the
steep field three times, and with flying yellow hair
and a diminishing shout rode up into the woods.

If she could have followed and found him then,
she would have started on foot. But she knew what
she would find when she would come to him. She
would find him equally real with herself—and
could not touch him then. As she was living and
inviolate, so of course was he, and when that gave
him delight, how could she bring a question to

him? She walked in the woods and around the graves in it, and knew about love, how it would have a different story in the world if it could lose the moral knowledge of a mystery that is in the other heart. Nothing in Floyd frightened her that drew her near, but at once she had the knowledge come to her that a fragile mystery was in everyone and in herself, since there it was in Floyd, and that whatever she did, she would be bound to ride over and hurt, and the secrecy of life was the terror of it. When Floyd rode the red horse, she lay in the grass. He might even have jumped across her. But the vaunting and prostration of love told her nothing—nothing at all.

The very next day Jenny waited on the stile and she saw Floyd come walking up the road in the morning, with drenched hair. He might have come and found her, but he came to the Lockhart house first.

The Lockhart house stood between two of the empty stretches along the road. It was wide, low, and twisted. Its roof, held up at the corners by the two chimneys, sagged like a hammock, and was mended with bark and small colored signs. The black high-water mark made a belt around the house and that alone seemed to tighten it and hold it together. Floyd stood gazing in at the doorway, as if what might not come out? And it was a beautiful doorway to see, with its fanlight and its sidelights, though they were blind with silt. The door was shut and the squirrels were asleep on the floor of the long cage across the front wall. Under the forward-tilting porch the clay-colored hens were sitting in twos in the old rowboat. And while Floyd looked, out came Mag.

And the next thing, he was playing with Mag Lockhart, that was an albino. Mag's short white hair would stream out from her head when she crouched nodding over her flowers in the yard, tending them with a jack-knife all day, and she would give a splitting laugh to see anyone come. Jenny from the stile watched them wrestle and play. The treadmill ran under the squirrels' quick feet.

Mag's voice came a long distance through the still day. "You are not!" "It is not!" "I am not!" she would scream, and she would jump away.

Floyd would turn on his heel and whirl old Mag off the ground. Mag ran and she snapped at him, she struggled and she crackled like a green wood fire, and he laughed and caught her. She pointed and sent him for the water, and he went and clattered and banged the buckets for her at the well until she begged him to stop. He went straight off and old Mag sat down on her front steps with the hens and rubbed at her flame-pink arms.

And then suddenly Mag was gone.

Jenny put her hands over her forehead, and then rubbed at her own arms. She believed Mag had been there, because she had felt whatever Mag had felt. If this was a vision, it was the first. And it did not frighten her; she knew it only came because she had felt what was in another heart besides her own. But it had been Mag's heart that grew clear to her, while Floyd ran away.

She lay down in the grass, which whispered in her ear. If desperation were only a country, it would be at the bottom of the well. She wanted to get there, to arrive graceful and airy in some strange other country and walk along its level land beneath its secret sky. She thought she could see herself, fleet as a mirror-image, rising up in a breath of astonished farewell and walking to the well of old Mag. It was built so that it had steps like a stile. She saw herself walk up them, stand on top, look about, and then go into the dark passage.

But my grandfather, she thought, even while she sank so deeply, will call me back. I will have to go back. He will ask me if I have put flowers on my mother's grave. And she looked over at the stone on the grave of her mother, with her married name of Lockhart cut into it.

She clutched the thing in her hand, a blade of grass, and held on. There she was, sitting up in the sun, with the blade of grass stretched between her thumbs and held to her mouth, for the calling back that was in the world. She blew on the grass. It made a thoughtless reedy sound, and she blew again.

II

The morning after her grandfather's death, Jenny put on a starched white dress and went down the hill into The Landing. A little crocheted bag hung by a ribbon over her wrist, and she had taken a nickel to put in it. Her good black strapped slippers moved lightly in the dust. She was going to tell the news of her grandfather, whom the old ladies had said would die suddenly —like *that*. And looking about with every step she took, she saw what a lonesome place it was for all of this to happen in.

She passed a house that only the mice inhabited. She passed a black boarded-up store where an owl used to live and maintain its nocturnal habits. And there, a young calf belonging to the Lockharts used to nose through the grassy rooms, before the walls were carried away by the Negroes and burned in a winter for firewood. In front of the row of Negro cabins was one long fence, made of lumber from old boats, built there to delay the river for one more moment when it came, the same as they would have delayed a giant bent on destruction by some foolish pretext.

Across the end of the road, crumbling under

her eyes, was a two-story building with a remnant
of gallery, and that was Jenny's destination. The
store and the postoffice were in the one used room.
Across the tin awning hung the moss icicles with
which the postmaster had decorated for Christ-
mas. Over the door was the shriveled mistletoe,
and the gun that had shot it down still standing
in the corner. Tipped back against the front wall
sat five old men in their chairs, with one holding
the white cat. On the step, Son Alford was playing his mandolin that had been Jenny's mother's
and given away. He was singing his fast song.

> *"Ain't she cute*
> *Ain't she smart*
> *Don't look twice*
> *It'll break my heart*
> *Everybody loves my gal."*

All nodded to her, but they knew she was not supposed to speak to them.

She went inside, and the first thing she saw was
Billy Floyd. He was standing in the back of the
room with the postmaster saying to him, "Reckon
we're going to have water this year?"

She had never seen the man between walls and
under a roof and somehow it made him a different
man after the one in the field. He stood in the dim
and dingy store with a row of filmy glass lamps
and a pair of boots behind his head, and there was

something close, gathering-close, and used and worldly about him.

"That slime, that's just as slick! You know how a fish is, I expect," the postmaster was saying affably to them both, just as if they were in any way together. "That's the way a house is, been under water. It's a sight to see those niggers try to clean this place out, falling down to slide from here to the front door and back. You have to get the slime off right away too, or you never can. Sure would make the best paint in the world." He laughed.

There was something handled and used about Floyd, something strong as an odor, the odor of the old playing cards that the old men of The Landing shuffled every day over their table in the street.

"Reckon we're going to have water this year?" the postmaster asked again. He looked from one of them to the other.

Floyd said nothing, he only held a penny. For a moment Jenny thought he was going to drop his high head at being trapped in the confined place, with her between him and the door, which would be the same as telling it out, before a third person, that he could be known in time if he were caught and cornered in a little store.

"What would you like today, Miss Jenny?" asked the postmaster. "Posy seeds?"

But she could not think what she would like.
She held her little bag quite still, the strings drawn
tight.

All the time, Floyd was giving her a glaring
look.

"Well, it makes you think sometimes, to see the
water come over all the world," said the postmaster. "I took everything I could out of here last
time. Then I come down from the hill and peeked
in the door and what did I see? My showcases com-
mencing to float loose. What a sight that did make!
I wouldn't have thought I sold some of them
things. Carried the showcases out on the hill, but
nowhere much to take them. Could you believe
I could carry everything out of my store in twenty
minutes but my safe? Couldn't lift that. Left the
door to it open and went off and left it. So as it
wouldn't rust shut, Floyd, Miss Jenny. Took me
a long time to scrape the river out of that thing."

All three waited a moment, and then the postmaster spoke again in a softer, intimate voice,
smilingly. "Some stranger lost through here says,
'Why don't you all move away?' Move away?" He
laughed, and pointed a finger at Jenny. "Did you
hear that, Miss Jenny—why don't we move away?
Because we live here, don't we, Miss Jenny?"

Then she knew it was a challenge Floyd made
with his hard look, and she lost to him. She walked
out and left him where he held his solid stand.

And when the postmaster had pointed his finger at her, she remembered that she was never to speak to Billy Floyd, by the order of her grandfather.

Outside the door, she stopped still. The weight of the nickel swung in her little bag, and she felt as if she had forgotten Doomsday. She took a step back toward the challenging Floyd. Then in a kind of haste she whispered to the five old men, separately, and even to Son Alford, and each time nearer to tears for her grandfather that died in the night. Then they gathered round her, and hurried her to the old women, and so back home.

But Floyd's face glared before her eyes all the way, it was like something in her vision that kept her from seeing. It was brighter than the glare of death. He might have been buying a box of matches with his penny, which was what his going cost. He would go. The danger of flood was her grandfather's dream, and the postmaster's storekeeper wit. These were bright days and clear nights; and so Floyd would not wait long in The Landing. That was what the old ladies said, and asked that their words be marked.

But on a later day, Jenny took a walk and met Floyd by the little river that came out of she spring and went to the Mississippi beyond. She sat down and made a clover chain that would never get long because the cloverheads slipped

out, and while she made it she kept looking with
assuring looks into his illuminated eyes that went
over the landscape and searched the sky for clouds.
She could hold his look for a moment and then it
would get away. She did not say a thing to him,
for nobody can say, "It is a heavy heart that makes
me clumsy." Nobody can say anything so true and
apologetic. Nobody can say, "Forgive the heavy
heart that loves more than the tongue can say or
the hands can do. Look back at me every time I
look at you and never feel pity, for what my heart
holds this minute is better than what you offer the
least bit less." Her eyes were telling him this but
if he knew it or felt a threat in it, he never gave
a sign. "My heart loves more than I can say or do,
but feel no pity, only have a little vision too, of
all clumsiness fallen away." She guessed that all
grace belongs to the future. But he never had anything to say to her thought or her guess. He stood
above her with his feet planted down and looked
out over the landscape from within that moment.
Level with him now, all The Landing spread
under his eyes. Not knowing the world around,
she could not know how The Landing looked set
down in it. All she knew was that he would leave
it when his patience gave out, and that this little
staving moment by the river would reach its limit
and go first.

Her eyes descended slowly, as if adorned with

flowers, from his light blowing hair and his gathering brows down, down him, past his clever hands that caught and trapped so delicately away from her side, softly down to the ground that was a sandy shore. A hidden mussel was blowing bubbles like a spring through the sand where his boot was teasing the water. It was the little pulse of bubbles and not himself or herself that was the moment for her then; and he could have already departed and she could have already wept, and it would have been the same, as she stared at the little fountain rising so gently out of the shimmering sand. A clear love is *in the world*—this came to her as insistently as the mussel's bubbles through the water. There it was, existing there where they came and were beside it now. It is in the bubble in the water in the river, and it has its own changing and its mysteries of days and nights, and it does not care how we come and go.

But when the moment ended, he went. And as soon as he left The Landing, the rain began to fall.

Each day the storm clouds were opening like great purple flowers and pouring out their dark thunder. Each nightfall, the storm was laid down on their houses like a burden the day had carried. The noise of rain, of the gullies filling, of the little river leaping up and running in waves filled all The Landing.

And when at last the river came, it did come like a hand and arm, and pushed black trees before it, but it was at dawn. Jenny went with the others, behind Mag Lockhart, onto the hill and the water followed, whirling and bobbing the young dead animals around on its roaring breast. The clouds lowered and broke again and the rain put out the lanterns. Boat whistles began crying as faint as baby cries in that rainy dark.

Jenny had not spoken for a day and a night on the hill when she told someone that she was sleepy. It was Billy Floyd that she told it to. He put her in his boat, that she had never seen. Jenny looked in Floyd's shining eyes and saw how they held the whole flood, as the flood held its triumph in its whirlpools, and it was a vast and unsuspected thing.

It was on the high hill of the cemetery, when the water was at its peak. They came in Floyd's boat where the river lapped around the dark cedar tops, and monuments like pillars to bear them up scraped their passage, and she knew they rode over the grave of her grandfather and the grave of her mother. Muscadine vines spread under the water rippling their leaves like schools of fishes. It was

always the same darkness. Fires burned some
where, but in the distance, red and blue.

"I . . ." she began, and stopped.

He scowled.

She knew at once that there was nothing in her
life past or even now in the flood that would make
anything to tell. He already knew that he had
saved her life, for that had taken up his time in
the time of danger. Yet she might confess it. It
came to her lips. He scowled on. Still, it was not
any kind of confession that she would finally wish
to make. She would like to tell him some strange
beautiful thing, if she could speak at all, something to make him speak. Communication would
be telling something that is all new, so as to have
more of the new told back. The dream of that
held her spellbound, with the things possible that
hung in the air like clouds over the world, and
she smiled in pure belief, for they were beautiful.

"I . . ." She looked softly at him as if from a
distance down a little road or a little tether he
sent her on.

He took hold of her, put her out of the boat
into a little place he made that was dry and green
and smelled good, and she went to sleep. After a
time that could have been long or short, she
thought she heard him say, "Wake up."

When her eyes were open and clear upon him,
he violated her and still he was without care or

demand and as gay as if he were still clanging the bucket at the well. With the same thoughtlessness of motion, that was a kind of grace, he next speared a side of wild meat from an animal he had killed and had ready in his boat, and cooked it over a fire he had burning on the ground. All the water lapped around. Over its sound she whispered something, but his movement and his task went on firmly about his leaping fire. People who had been there in other floods had put their initials on the tree. Her words came a little louder and in shyness she changed them from words of love to words of wishing, but still he did not look around. "I wish you and I could be far away. I wish for a little house." But ideas of any different thing from what was in his circle of fire might never have reached his ears, for all the attention he paid to her remarks.

He had fishes ready too, wrapped and cooking in a hole scooped in the ground. When she ate it was in obedience to him, though he did not say "Eat" or say anything, he only smiled at the fire, and for him it was all a taking freely of what was free. She knew from him nevertheless that what people ate in the world was earth, river, wildness and litheness, fire and ashes. People took the fresh death and the hot fire into their mouths and got their own life. She ate greedily as long as he ate, and took what he took. She ate eagerly, looking up at him while her teeth bit, to show him herself, her proud hunger, as if to please and flatter him with her original and now lost starvation. But she could make him neither sorry nor proud. When she was sick afterwards, he walked away and waited apart from her shame, as he had left her in his delight.

The dream of love, that made her hold as still in her life as if she heard music, had never carried her yet to the first country of which it told. But there was a country, as surely as there was herself. When she saw the moon come up that night and grow bright as it went above the flood and the boats in it, she was not as sorrowful as she might have been, now that they floated so high, that no threads hung down from the moon, no tender ladder all at once caught light and drifted down. There was a need in all dreams for something to stay far, far away, never to torment with the rest, and the bright moon now was that.

III

When the water was down, Jenny went back below and Floyd went down the river in his boat. They parted with the clumsiest of touches. Down through the exhausted and still dripping trees she made her way, again behind Mag, following the tracks and signs of others, and the mud sticking

to her. Ashes sifted through the air and she saw
them touch her skin but did not feel them. She
came to the stile where she could look at the world
below. The sun was going down and a wind blew
following after the river, and the little town had
turned the color of river water and the trees in
their shame of refuse rattled like yellow pebbles
and the houses sank below them scuffed and small.
The smoky band of woods that lay in the distance
toward the retreating river still seemed to waver
and slide.

In The Landing the houses had turned a little,
like people whose skirts are pulled. Where the
front of the Lockhart house had been pulled away,
the furniture, that had been carried out of the
corners by the river and rocked about, stood in the
middle of the floor and showed down its back the
curly yellow grain, like its long hair. One old store
had been carried clean away, after it was closed so
long, and in its foundations were the old men
standing around poking for money with little
sticks. Money could have fallen through the cracks
for many years. Fifteen cents and twenty cents
and a Spanish piece were found, and the old fel-
lows poking with their sticks were laughing like
women.

Jenny came to her house. It stood as before, except that in the yellow and windy light it seemed
to draw its galleries to itself, to return to its cave

of night and trees, crouched like a child going backwards to the womb.

But once inside, she took one step and was into a whole new ecstasy, an ecstasy of cleaning, to wash the river out. She ran as if driven, carrying buckets and mops. She scrubbed and pried and shook the river away. Even the pages of books seemed to have been opened and written on again by muddy fingers. In the long days when she stretched and dried white curtains and sheets, rubbed the rust off knives and made them shine, and wiped the dark river from all the prisms, she forgot even love, to clean.

But the shock of love had brought a trembling to her fingers that made her drop what she touched, and made her stumble on the stair, though all the time she was driven on. And when the house was clean again she felt that there was no place to hide in it, not one room. She even opened the small door of her mother's last room, but when she looked in she thought of her mother who was kept guard on there, who struggled unweariedly and all in loneliness, and it was not a hiding place.

If in all The Landing she could have found a place to feel alone and out of sight, she would have gone there. One old lady or another would always call to her when she went by, to tell her something, and if she walked out in the road she brushed up against the old men sitting at their cards, and they spoke to her. She did not like to see faces, which were ugly, or flowers, which were beautiful and smelled sweet.

But at last the trembling left and dull strength came back, as if a wound had ceased to flow its blood. And then one day in summer she could look at a bird flying in the air, its tiny body like a fist opening and closing, and did not feel daze or pain, and then she was healed of the shock of love.

Then whenever she thought that Floyd was in the world, that his life lived and had this night and day, it was like discovery once more and again fresh to her, and if it was night and she lay stretched on her bed looking out at the dark, a great radiant energy spread intent upon her whole body and fastened her heart beneath its breath, and she would wonder almost aloud, "Ought I to sleep?" For it was love that might always be coming, and she must watch for it this time and clasp it back while it clasped, and while it held her never let it go.

Then the radiance touched at her heart and her brain, moving within her. Maybe some day she could become bright and shining all at once, as though at the very touch of another with herself. But now she was like a house with all its rooms dark from the beginning, and someone would have to go slowly from room to room, slowly and darkly, leaving each one lighted behind, before going to the next. It was not caution or distrust that was in herself, it was only a sense of journey, of something that might happen. She herself did not know what might lie ahead, she had never seen herself. She looked outward with the sense of rightful space and time within her, which must be traversed before she could be known at all. And what she would reveal in the end was not herself, but the way of the traveler.

In The Landing much was known about all kinds of love that had happened there, and wisdom traveled, when it left the porches, in the persons of three old women. The day the old women would come to see Jenny, it would be to celebrate her ruin that they trudged through the sun in their bonnets. They would come up the hill to say, "Why don't you run after him?" and to say, "Now you won't love him any more," for they always did pay a visit to say those words.

Now only Mag came sidling up, and brought a bouquet of amaryllis to present with blushes to Jenny. Jenny blushed too.

"Some people that don't speak to other people don't grow the prettiest flowers!" Mag cried victoriously as Jenny took them. Her baby hair blew down and her sharp smile cut back into her long dry cheek.

"I speak to you, Mag," said Jenny.

When she walked she heard them talk—the three old ladies. About her they said, "She'll follow her mother to her mother's grave." About Floyd they had more to say. They called him "the wild man" because they had never been told quite who he was or where he had come from. The sun had burned his skin dark and his hair light, till he was golden in the road, and they freely considered his walking by again, as if they could take his life up into their fingers with their sewing and sew it or snip it on their laps. They always went back to saying that at any rate he caught enormous fish wherever he fished in the river, and always had a long wet thing slung over his wrist when he went by, ugh! One old lady thought he was a Gipsy and had called "Gipsy!" after him when he went by her front porch once too often. One lady said she did not care what he was or if she ever knew what he was, and whether he lived or died it was all the same to her. But the third old lady had books, though she was the one that was a little crazy, and she waited till the others had done and then explained that Floyd had the blood of a Natchez Indian, though the Natchez might be supposed to be all gone, massacred. The Natchez, she said—and she nodded toward her books, "The Queen's Library," high on the shelf—were the people from the lost Atlantis, had they heard of that? and took their pride in the escape from that flood, when the island went under. And there was something all Indians knew, about never letting the last spark of fire go out. What did the other ladies think of that?

They were shocked. They had thought all the time he was really the bastard of one of the old checker-players, that had been let grow up away in the woods until he got big enough to come back and make trouble. They said he was half-wild like one family they could name, and half of the time he did not know what he was doing, like another family. All in his own right he could scent coming things like an animal and in some of his ways, just like all men, he was something of an animal. But they said it was the way he was.

"Why don't you run after him?"—"Now you won't love him any more."

Jenny wondered what more love would be like. Then of course she knew. More love would be quiet. She would never be so quiet as she wished until she was quiet with her love. In the center of everything, in the center of thunder, there was a precious piece of quiet, and into quiet her love would go. The Landing was filled with clangor, it seemed to her, until her love was filled with quiet. It seemed to her that she had been the same as in many places in the world, traveling and traveling, always with quiet to give. It had been enough to

make her desperate in her heart, the long search
for Billy Floyd to give quiet to.

But if Floyd had a search, what was it?

She was holding the amber beads they used to
give her mother to play with. She looked at the
lump of amber, and looked through to its core.
Nobody could ever know about the difference between the radiance that was the surface and the
radiance that was inside. There were the two
worlds. There was no way at all to put a finger
on the center of light. And if there were a moun-
tain, the cloud over it could not touch its heart
when it traveled over, and if there were an island
out in the sea, the waves at its shore would never
come over the place in the middle of the island.
She looked in her very dreams at Floyd who had
such clear eyes shining at her, and knew his heart
lay clearer still, safe and deep in his innocence,
safe and away from the outside, deeper than quiet.
What she remembered was that when her hand
started out to touch him in delight, he smiled and
turned away—not from her, but toward something. . . .

Was it toward one thing, toward some one thing
alone?

But it was when love was of the one for the one,
that it seemed to hold all that was multitudinous
and nothing was single any more. She had one love
and that was all, but she dreamed that she lined

up on both sides of the road to see her love come by in a procession. She herself was more people than there were people in The Landing, and her love was enough to pass through the whole night, never lifting the same face.

It was July when Jenny left The Landing. The grass was tall and gently ticking between the tracks of the road. The stupor of air, the quiet of the river that now went behind a veil, the sheen of heat and the gray sheen of summering trees, and the silence of day and night seemed all to touch, to bathe and administer to The Landing. The little town took a languor and a kind of beauty from the treatment of time and place. It stretched and swooned, and when two growing boys knelt in the road and caught the sun rays in a bit of glass and got fire, they seemed to tease a sleeper, and when they said "Hooray!" they sounded like adventurers in a dream.

Pears lying on the ground warmed and soured, bees gathered at the figs, birds put their little holes of possession in each single fruit in the world that they could fly to. The scent of lilies rolled sweetly from their heavy cornucopias and trickled down by shady paths to fill the golden air of the valley. The mourning dove called its three notes, kept its short silence—which was its mourning?— and called three more.

Jenny had known the most when she knew Floyd rode the horse in the field of butterflies while she was still; and she had known something when she watched him cook the meat and had eaten it for him under his eye; and now once more, in the dream of July, she knew very little, she was lost in wonder again. If she could find him now, or even find the place where he had last passed through, she would gain the next wisdom. It was a following after, now—it was too late to find any way alone.

The sun was going down when she went. The red eyes of the altheas were closing, and the lizards ran on the wall. The last lily buds hung green and glittering, pendulant in the heat. The crape-myrtle trees were beginning to fill with light for they drank the last of it every day, and gave off their white and flame in the evening that filled with the throb of cicadas. There was an old mimosa closing in the ravine—the ancient fern, as old as life, the tree that shrank from the touch, grotesque in its tenderness. All nearness and darkness affected it, even clouds going by, but for Jenny that left it no tree ever gave such allurement of fragrance anywhere.

She looked behind her for the last time as she went down under the trees. As if it were made of shells and pearls and treasures from the sea, the house glinted in the sunset, tinted with the drops of light that seemed to fall slowly through the vaguely stirring leaves. Tenderly as seaweed the long moss swayed. The chimney branched like coral in the upper blue.

Then green branches closed it over, and with her next step trumpet and muscadine vines and the great big-leaved vines made pillars about the trunks of the trees and arches and buttresses all among them. Passion flowers bloomed with their white and purple rays about her shoulders and under her feet. She walked on into the streaming hot shade of the wilderness, and put out her hands between the hanging vines. She feared the snakes in the sudden cool. Like thousands of silver bells the frogs rang her through the swamp, which then closed behind her.

All at once the whole open sky could be seen— she had come to the river. A quiet fire burned on the bluff and moving as far outward as she could see was the cold blur of water. A great spiraled net lay on its side and its circles twinkled faintly on the sky. Veil behind veil of long drying nets hung on all sides, dropping softly and blue-colored in the low wind and the place was folded in by them. All things, river, sky, fire, and air, seemed the same color, the color that is seen behind the closed eyelids, the color of day when vision and despair are the same thing.

Some fishermen came around her and when she

named Billy Floyd they nodded their heads. They said, what with the rains, they waited for the racing of the waters to slow down, but that he went out on them. They said he was out on them now, but would come back to the camp, if he did not turn over and drown first. She asked the fishermen to let her wait there with them, since it was to them that he would return. They said it did not matter to them how long she waited, or where.

She stood by the nets. A little distance away men and women were cooking and eating and she smelled the fish and the wild meat. The river went by immeasurable under the sky, moving and dimly catching and snagging itself, freeing itself without effort, heavy with its great waves of drift, deep with stirring fish.

But after a certain length of time, the men that had been throwing knives at the tree by the last light put her inside a grounded houseboat on the plank of which chickens were standing. The willow branches hung down over and dragged softly back and forth across the roof. There were noises and fires all around. There were pigs in the wood.

One by one the men came in to her. She actually spoke to the first one that entered between the dozing chickens, for now she could speak to everyone, in a vague stir of welcome or in the humility that moved now deep in her spirit. About them all and closer to them than their own breath was the smell of trees that had bled to the knives they wore.

When she called out, she did not call any name; it was a cry with a rising sound, as if she said "Go back," or asked a question, and then at the last protested. A rude laugh covered her cry, and somehow both the harsh human sounds could easily have been heard as rejoicing, going out over the river in the dark night. By the fire, little boys were slapped crossly by their mothers—as if they knew that the original smile now crossed Jenny's face, and hung there no matter what was done to her, like a bit of color that kindles in the sky after the light has gone.

"Is she asleep? Is she in a spell? Or is she dead?" asked a little old bright-eyed woman who went and looked in the door, and crept up to the now meditating men outside. She was so precise in her question that she even held up three rheumatic fingers when she asked.

"She's waiting for Billy Floyd," they said.

The old woman nodded, and nodded out to the flowing river, with the firelight following her face and showing its dignity. The younger boys separated and took their turns throwing knives with a dull *pit* at the tree.

Books by Eudora Welty
available in Harvest paperback editions from
Harcourt Brace & Company

THE BRIDE OF THE INNISFALLEN AND OTHER STORIES

THE COLLECTED STORIES OF EUDORA WELTY

A CURTAIN OF GREEN AND OTHER STORIES

DELTA WEDDING

THE GOLDEN APPLES

THE PONDER HEART

THE ROBBER BRIDEGROOM

THIRTEEN STORIES

THE WIDE NET AND OTHER STORIES